The Serious Game

The Serious Game

HJALMAR SÖDERBERG

Translated from the Swedish
by Eva Claeson

MARION BOYARS PUBLISHERS LTD
LONDON • NEW YORK

Published in Great Britain and the United States
in 2001 by MARION BOYARS PUBLISHERS
24 Lacy Road, London SW15 1NL
237 E 39th Street, New York NY 10016

Originally published in Sweden in 1912
under the title *Den Allvarsamma Leken*

www.marionboyars.co.uk

Distributed in Australia and New Zealand by
Peribo Pty Ltd, 58 Beaumont Road, Kuring-gai, NSW

Printed in 2001
10 9 8 7 6 5 4 3 2 1

Elena Balzamo's 'Toying With Happiness: An Introduction to Hjalmar Söderberg's *The Serious Game*' was first published in 1995 as 'Les Jeux du Bonheur' in *Le Jeux Sérieux*

The Publishers would like to thank the Embassy of Sweden for a translation grant from the Bernard Shaw fund.

A CIP catalogue record for this book is available from the British Library.
A CIP catalog record for this book is available from the Library of Congress.

ISBN 0-7145-3061-1
Printed in Great Britain by Cox & Wyman, Reading, Berkshire

TOYING WITH HAPPINESS

An Introduction to Hjalmar Söderberg's *The Serious Game*

By Elena Balzamo

In 1912 Hjalmar Söderberg, already a celebrated and controversial author, published a new novel: *The Serious Game*. At the age of forty-three he had produced three novels, as many collections of stories, two plays, an essay and an innumerable amount of critical writing. *The Serious Game*, the longest, most ambitious and perhaps the most successful of his works, was not only the crowning achievement of Söderberg's literary career, one that had stretched back over fifteen years, but also suggested new possibilities to the author. Who at the time would have suspected that this novel, which bore witness to an artistic talent in the full flowering of his abilities, would also be his swan song: the raising of a creative voice that would lead to silence? This, however, was to be the case. In the thirty years that remained of his life, Söderberg produced nothing to equal his earlier works: in fact, he would no longer write fiction, abandoning literature in favour of history and religion. The publication of *The Serious Game* was followed by six years of total silence, just as the previous six years had seen him produce the vast majority of his most important writings. The causes of this silence and the slowing down of his artistic output can be found in the events that had overturned Söderberg's life during this period, completely altering its course.

Out of his entire, somewhat uneventful life, the period from 1903 to 1912 is highlighted by the intense dramas it encompassed. In 1903, after four years of disastrous marriage to an emotionally unstable woman, Hjalmar Söderberg received a letter from an unknown female, expressing her admiration for *The Youth of Martin Birck*, the novel he wrote in 1901. A young woman, the wife of an officer, sensitive, fond of literature, languishing in the colourless provinces beside her ageing husband, had entered Söderberg's life. Her name was Maria von Platen. An exchange of letters ensued, followed by a meeting, and Söderberg was soon involved in an affair the outcome of which he was still unable to foresee. A tumultuous three-year relationship punctuated by varying periods of separation and reconciliation began in 1903. Söderberg would go back to her on numerous occasions. However, for Maria von Platen, who went on to have affairs with other Swedish men of letters, this affair was just another simple episode. For Hjalmar Söderberg, in his 'search for happiness', it was to become a terrifying drama, a catastrophe that stripped him of everything. Ground down by the fighting at home, the scandal that surrounded him after the affair became public, the anguish caused by his break-up with a wife whom he still loved and his mounting financial problems, he could see only one solution: flight.

'I know that I scarcely had a choice,' he explained in a letter. 'The extreme solution was at hand.' Could he have suspected that by leaving Sweden in 1906 he was condemning himself to an eternal exile? That by cutting himself off from the nurturing womb-like environment of Stockholm he was signing his own death warrant? By no means, even if he did claim to have reached a crossroads in both his personal life and his literary career. 'I only went to Copenhagen for a brief stay. I had no plans. I saw no future ahead of me... I considered myself finished as a writer.'

And so it was that after a slight moment's hesitation he settled in Copenhagen and became involved with a young Danish woman, who would bear him a child in 1910 and became his second wife in 1917. He was to enjoy a peaceful and orderly existence with her until his death in 1941, never to return to Sweden except on short visits.

But all of this lay in the future. In 1906, uprooted, battered and penniless, Hjalmar Söderberg disembarked in Copenhagen, moved into a small hotel and fought his first battle with the demons that were tormenting him. The result was *Gertrud*, the play that became famous throughout Europe thanks to Carl Dreyer's film adaptation. First published in 1906, it had already enjoyed productions in both Stockholm and Copenhagen by 1907. The play, which drew upon certain aspects of his experiences with Maria von Platen, without reproducing them exactly, was centred entirely upon the character of Gertrud, a woman who could only exist for – and through – love. It was not, however, a settling of old scores with his former mistress, but rather an act of total absolution. A single desire had survived Hjalmar Söderberg's grand passion: to understand. 'I believe I would like to be something that most likely doesn't exist,' says Arvid Stjärnblom, the male protagonist of *The Serious Game*. 'I would like to be "the soul of the world". To be the one who knows and understands everything.'

Despite the undeniable success of *Getrud*, and the cathartic effect it must have had upon its creator, its subject matter was far from being exhausted. The demons from the past continued to crowd in, and Söderberg would make another attempt to exorcise them: this time in *The Serious Game*.

Hjalmar Söderberg has the well-earned reputation of being one of the poet laureates of Stockholm's city life, due in part to the portrait he presents of it in *The Serious Game*. Nearly every district of the Swedish capital is described here, unencumbered by too much detail but captured with a striking clarity as a series of 'snapshots' in which permanent details, such as houses, gardens and churches, are set against other, more ephemeral elements: atmospheric conditions, changes in light, the flow of crowds… Stockholm at the start of the twentieth century is revealed to us as a living, moving thing, its features changing with the passing of time. Automobiles replace horse-drawn cabs; gas lamps make way for electric lighting. At first glance, there's nothing surprising about this: a realist author describing a place he knows well, which has been a familiar part of his daily life and which he knows right down to its smallest detail. However, the suggestive power with which Stockholm is evoked is due less to the fact that it was once the writer's natural locale, than that it has ceased to be so. *The Serious Game* is a novel composed in exile: by the time it was being written, Söderberg had definitively left the country of his birth behind him. Everything he describes – the cafés, the nights at the Opera, the walks along the quays – belonged to the past, to an era that, like his youth, was now gone for good.

'But if you were a poet,' Arvid, the protagonist of *The Serious Game* is asked by Lydia, his lover, 'could you not then, like Goethe and Strindberg and so many other and lesser ones, make "literature" from what was once, for you, life and reality, happiness and unhappiness? Couldn't you?' 'Never,' he replies. 'I don't think that it's possible, even for a poet for that matter, to make literature from his love so long as there's the spark of life in it. I suppose it has to be dead first, before he can embalm it.' This exchange reveals, beyond the problematic relationship between fiction and reality, one of the most frequently recurring themes in Söderberg's writing, precisely delineating the author's attitude towards the description of events. His time in Stockholm was over; the drama played out. The past was now dead. 'I have come more and more to realise that I can never bring it back to life,' he announced in a letter written as early as 1907: the wheels of artistic creation had been set in motion. The trauma that he lived through had become nothing more than raw material ready to be transformed into a work of art. 'It is not what he has experienced that is the cause for all that is sick, horrible and confused in his writing,' Arvid Stjärnblom observes of Strindberg in *The Serious Game*. 'That's what he seems to believe himself, but that's not the way it is. On the contrary, it is all that is sick, horrible and confused in his own nature that causes everything he has to experience and live through.' This observation is particularly apt. Refracted through the prism of Söderberg the Artist, the emotional drama that pitched Söderberg the Man into a state of total chaos transforms itself into a marvellously balanced literary work. The disruptive experience is still there, but restructured and, for want of a better word, put in its place.

Some Swedish critics accused Söderberg of incorporating into his narrative 'digressions' and 'collages' that had no direct relevance to its emotional conflicts. One has only to compare *The Serious Game* with *Gertrud* to understand the function of this material. In Söderberg's play the outside world doesn't exist: nothing is real except the relationships between the characters. *The Serious Game*'s romantic complications, however, take place against the political intrigues of the world. The 'affairs' that shook Sweden at the time are integrated into an exceptionally broad tableau: the Dreyfus Affair, the troubled Union between Norway and Sweden, theological debates, the encroaching shadow of world war. This approach has a dual effect. Primarily, it introduces a sense of scale into Arvid's emotional drama, little more than a grain of sand tossed about in the global tempest. At the same time, the drama acquires an objective existence: the protagonist's sufferings over his mistress become, in their own right, a part of human history: the drama and sufferings of every individual. From this develops the frequently disturbing impression of the characters' physical existence: their presence in reality. One curious result of this effect was the publication in 1969 – more than half a century after *The Serious Game* first appeared – of the novel *For Lydia*, whose author, G. Sundström, retells the same story from the heroine Lydia's point of view instead.

Arvid Stjärnblom is, without doubt, one of Söderberg's most compelling creations. This provincial youth, like Rastignac in Balzac's *Le Père Goriot*, comes to Stockholm with the intention of conquering it but, unlike his French predecessor, refuses success attained at any price. Here is another moral being akin to

Martin Birck, the protagonist of Söderberg's second novel, whose intransigence upsets his parents and consigns him to an isolated and despairing existence, or Dr Glas, eponymous hero of another Söderberg novel who – always in the name of moral scruples – becomes a murderer. Once more a moral conscience fails to bring happiness. 'I have always imagined that honesty and a certain disinterested love of truth were two of my most important traits. Now I find myself in situations that make falsehood, trickery and lies almost daily necessities, and I realise to my surprise that I have talents in those realms as well,' Arvid Stjärnblom tells himself, and once again we can detect the voice of the author himself speaking. In reality, the character is deluding himself. In his slide from falsehood to falsehood, sometimes requiring caution, sometimes pity, sometimes fear, he sets himself upon a path to nowhere – an impasse from which he cannot escape without abandoning everything he had formerly relied upon for his existence: love, career, social standing, family.

Fifteen years of such slow attrition suddenly climax in a resounding defeat: the hero flees, just as his creator did, weary and disheartened, without any plan for his future. Where does the fault lie? In that moment of defiance at the start of the novel, where the hero condemns himself by refusing to become 'tied down' to the girl that he nonetheless loves? It's a fault for which he is immediately made to pay over and over again, and Stjärnblom's wasted existence is certainly not the punishment for his youthful weakness.

The Serious Game is the most fatalistic of Söderberg's novels, drawing upon the repeated defeats incurred by the author in his attempts at 'being happy'. 'We scarcely know what seeds we sow,' he had already remarked in his first novel, *Aberrations*. 'We cannot assume responsibility for whatever happens. We cannot go forward, or retrace our steps or even stay where we are.' Later, this theme is taken up and developed further in *The Youth of Martin Birck*: Schopenhauer's image of the 'human marionette' exactly reflects what the author thought of the concept of free will. It is an idea echoed throughout Söderberg's many novels. Reinforced by the passing of the years, it was to become the main theme of *The Serious Game*: 'You do not choose your destiny, any more than you choose your wife, your lover or your children. You get them, and you have them, and possibly you lose them. But you don't choose them!' And so it happens that the most active and wilful of Söderberg's characters, Arvid Stjärnblom, is as incapable of controlling his own destiny as the others, unable to escape an unhappy marriage or retain the love of his mistress. In vain does he try to peer ahead and take precautions: things 'happen'. The best he can do is to take the blows with dignity.

The fatal love that becomes Arvid Stjärnblom's destiny is woven from acts of betrayal. The first, committed by the hero himself, remains almost innocent. Later, the wounds that the characters inflict upon each other become more and more calculated and deliberate. Such betrayals are inevitable because the veils that prevent these individuals from truly seeing themselves are never really lifted. Despite their many attempts at explanation, no one completely frees themselves. 'I believe in the desire of the flesh and the irremediable solitude of the spirit': Söderberg's most famous statement is the perfect encapsulation of his greatest novel. In *The Serious Game*, this fatalistic view of existence is exacerbated. Consequently, the book does not just encapsulate the personal experiences of its author and draw a line under his 'personal life' – the novel's narrative extends into 1912, the year when it was written – it is also the summation of his intellectual quest and a conclusion to his earlier work. Even while maintaining a fair sense of proportion, it is possible to describe *The Serious Game* as a 'total' novel and, thanks to its success, a true moment of completion.

'*The Serious Game*,' declared one critic in the 1930s, 'is the only love story that stands for anything in our literature.' Not everyone would agree with this statement, but no one would deny that, after its guarded welcome from the press of the day, due as much to the book itself as the author's controversial personality, the novel quickly attained the status it enjoys today: that of a literary classic. *The Serious Game* has gone through numerous editions, has been adapted for the screen, the subject of much research and translated into several languages. However, everything seems to have been said about the novel back in 1913 by Bo Bergman, the poet and Hjalmar Söderberg's friend: 'It is not just a precious jewel of refined intelligence and stylistic control. It is the work of a grown man, coming from the heart and soul, and with all the colours of life.'

Chartres, June 1994

Translated from the French by Ken Hollings

PART I

'I can't bear the idea
of someone waiting for me...'

As usual, Lydia went swimming alone.

She liked it best that way. Besides, she had no one to go swimming with that summer. She had no need to worry: her father, who always sat on a nearby rock painting his 'Coastal Motif', kept a close eye on her and saw to it that no stranger came too near.

She waded out until the water reached a little above her waist, then waited with raised arms, her hands clasped behind her head, until the rings in the water smoothed out again and reflected her eighteen-year-old body in the shallow waves.

Then she bent forward and swam out over the emerald-green deep. She enjoyed the feeling of the water bearing her – she felt so light. She swam with calm, measured strokes. She didn't see any perch today. Sometimes she played with them. Once, she was so close to catching one that she pricked her hand on its fins.

Back on land she ran the towel over her body quickly, then stretched out on a flat rock that had been worn smooth by the waves and let the sun and the light summer breeze dry her. First she lay on her stomach to let the sun shine on her back. Her whole body was very tanned already – as tanned as her face.

She let her thoughts wander. She thought about the fact that it was almost noon. They were going to have fried ham and spinach. She looked forward to it, even though lunch was always the most boring part of the day. Her father never said much, and her brother Otto just sat there, sullen and silent. Of course, he did have problems. He wanted to become an engineer but there were already too many engineers here at home, so he was leaving for the United States in the autumn. The only one who said anything at all was Philip, but what he said never interested her

– he talked about precedents and legal strategies and promotions and other such nonsense that no one could be interested in. It was as though he talked just for the sake of talking, all the while searching with his near-sighted eyes for the best morsels on the platter.

Actually, she was very fond of her father and her brothers. Strange that sitting at the table with the people closest to you could be so unpleasant…

She turned on her back, supported her head on her hands and looked up into the blue.

Blue skies, white clouds, she thought. Blue and white… I have a blue dress with white lace on it. It's my best dress, but that's not why I like it so much. There's another reason. It's the dress I wore that time.

That time.

I wonder whether he loves me? Yes, of course he does.

But does he really love me – really?

She remembered that time not so long ago, when they were sitting alone together in the lilac arbour. He had suddenly attempted a rather daring caress that had frightened her. But then he had immediately realized that he had gone too far, had taken her hand, the very hand she had used to ward him off, and had kissed it, as if to say: I'm sorry.

Her thoughts were so real that her lips were moving, and she found herself whispering: I love him.

Blue and white – blue and white…and the splashing of the water – splash – splash…

Suddenly it occurred to her that she had only realized that summer how wonderful it was to swim alone. She wondered why. It did feel good. When girls went swimming together they always shouted and laughed and made such a noise. It was much nicer to be alone and completely silent and to listen to the splashing of the water against the rocks.

While dressing she hummed a tune:

Together one day we'll stand
before the priest,
and you will take my hand,
to keep forever till time has ceased.

But she didn't sing the words. She only hummed the melody.

Mr Stille, the painter, had since time immemorial rented the same red fisherman's cottage on an island far out in the Stockholm archipelago. He painted pine trees. They used to say that he had discovered the island pine, just as Edward Bergh had discovered the northern Swedish birch grove. He preferred his pines in sunshine after rain, with the trunks still wet and glistening. But he needed neither rain nor sunshine: he knew it all by heart. He also enjoyed painting the red reflections of the evening sun on the thin, pale-red bark at the tops of the trees and on the twisted, knotty branches. In the sixties he had been awarded a medal in Paris. His most famous pine hung in the Galleries du Luxembourg and he also had a couple of paintings at the National Museum. Now, at the end of the nineties, he was way over sixty and had gradually retreated into obscurity as a result of increasing competition. However, he continued to work steadily and diligently, as he had during his whole hard life, and he was still quite successful in selling his pine trees.

'There's no great art to painting,' he would say. 'Forty years ago I was just as good as I am now, but selling, that's where the art is, and mastering that takes time.'

His secret was simple: he sold cheap, and, as a result, he had managed quite well. What with a wife and three children he had done all right. He'd been a widower for several years now. Short, wiry and knotty with a bit of healthy skin showing here and there through his bushy beard, he looked like an old island pine himself.

Painting was his occupation; but music was his love. There had been a time when he had made fiddles for the pleasure of it and he had dreamed of discovering the long-forgotten secrets of violin making. With his pipe hanging out of a corner of his mouth, he still enjoyed playing at the Saturday evening dances on the island.

And he was delighted when he was asked to sing second bass in quartets. That was the reason he was in such a good mood at lunch that day.

'There's going to be singing tonight,' he said. 'Baron Freutiger phoned to say he'd be coming over together with Arvid Stjärnblom and Mr Lovén.'

The baron owned a small estate across the bay and was their nearest neighbour, except for the local fishermen, that is. Arvid Stjärnblom, who was a student, and Mr Lovén, a notary, were his guests.

Her cheeks burning, Lydia hastily left the table to get something from the kitchen.

'I'm not going to sing,' Philip muttered.

'Don't then,' their father grunted.

Actually, there was something wrong with the quartet: there were two first tenors. Old man Stille was a fine second bass. The baron professed that he could sing any part 'with equally brilliant wretchedness', and had decided to sing first bass. Arvid Stjärnblom sang second tenor, but the honour and responsibility of singing first tenor had to be shared by Philip and Mr Lovén. Philip's tenor was light and clear: decidedly lyrical. Lovén's on the other hand was colossal, and Philip's delicate voice didn't have a chance. It was said that he had been offered a job at the Opera. All the same, Philip was proud of the fact that he was indispensable for the more subtle passages, since his rival had only two strings to play on: forte and fortissimo. Besides, Mr Lovén had a major enemy: when under the influence of great emotion his voice cracked and sometimes he even sang off key.

Otto broke the silence.

'I bet you'll change your mind. I've never heard of a tenor who can keep his mouth shut when he hears others sing.'

'You can sing the parts that suit your voice,' their father said.

Philip sulked and picked at his spinach. He was thinking that he might possibly condescend to sing 'Why Are You So Far Away?' and perhaps some other popular song. He remembered the last time they had sung 'Why...?'. Lovén had boomed ahead, and then all of a sudden the baron had hit the punch tray with his tuning fork and said: 'Shut up, Lovén and let Philip sing this. He knows how!' And he remembered how very beautifully he had sung that time.

Lydia returned to the table.

'I found out what we're going to have for supper,' she said. 'It'll be ham again, and herring, and potatoes and Otto's perch. That's all there is.'

'And brandy and beer, and arrack and cognac,' Otto added.

'Fine! We don't need any more than that,' old man Stille said. 'Those are all wonderful gifts from God!'

The late-August sun was already setting when the baron's small sailboat rounded the point. The wind had subsided. The sails were slack, and they were rowing. As they approached, they lowered the sails and stopped rowing. The baron struck the note with his tuning fork and, while rocking gently on the waves, the three men in the boat broke into a Bellman trio.

Still'd is the hasty wave,
Aeolus is dying,
As from the shore he hears
Mandolins replying;
Where moonshine's lying
Cool and calm the water gleams.

Lilac and jasmine
fragrance lend the moonlight's beams.
Butterflies gold and green
here on a flower are seen,
Soon will the earthy worm
his dwelling flee.

The song rang out clear and beautiful across the water. Two old fishermen who were laying out lines in the bay stopped their work to listen.

'Bravo!' old man Stille shouted from the dock.

'That was pretty good, Lovén,' the baron said, 'except for that part about the worm. Philip's voice is better for that. Well, hello, everybody! How's everything, old man? Do you have any cognac? We've got the whisky. Ah, good evening, you dear, beautiful, sweet little Miss Lydia!' he said, and gallantly accompanied each expression of admiration by blowing Lydia a kiss. 'And good evening to you, boys!'

Baron Freutiger had a weather-beaten face with a full black beard. He was close to fifty but had kept his youth by taking life easy. Grief and worry had run off him without leaving a trace. Nevertheless, he had been through a lot and he used to say that one of his worst experiences had been when he was hanged for stealing a horse in Arizona. It was certainly true that he had been his family's black sheep and had tried his luck in many parts of the world. He was a jack-of-all-trades. He had published travel books that were so fresh and charmingly full of fabrications that he had become famous in literary circles, and he had composed waltzes that were danced to at royal functions. A few years ago he had come into an inheritance and had bought the small estate in the archipelago where, posing as a farmer, he now spent his time hunting sea birds and girls. He was also interested in politics. At the most recent election he had been a candidate for Parliament and would most likely have been voted in if he had understood the importance of expressing a more definite view on the subject of temperance.

Dressed in a snow-white flannel suit and with an old dirty straw hat of indeterminate shape perched on his head, he hopped on to the dock and was followed by the others from the boat. Mr Lovén, the public notary who worked for customs, a man of stately build, weather-beaten, somewhat plump and pretty like a doll, struck a pose and emitted a few high notes experimentally. Stjärnblom, the student, a broad-shouldered young man whose eyes were deep and reserved, remained in the background. Old man Stille and Philip joined them, the baron struck the note and, to the tones of 'The Raising of the Singers' Banner', the procession walked up to the red cottage, where, through the foliage of the small, vine-enclosed veranda, bottles and glasses could be seen shining in the light of the evening sun.

It was getting darker and darker now, and Capella, the bright August star, was already shining in the pale northern sky.

Lydia was leaning against the veranda railing. She had spent most of the evening running back and forth between the kitchen and the veranda carrying 'pots', her general name for bottles and glasses and other household utensils. She had waited on the men all by herself – Augusta, their old servant for the past twelve years, hissed like an angry cat whenever they had company, and refused to leave the kitchen.

And now Lydia was a little tired.

Song after song had resounded in the stillness of the evening, alternating here and there with the tenors' arguments, which were always settled by the clinking of glasses filled with three different sorts of refreshing drinks. Now the singers were sitting talking peacefully. At the railing, Lydia looked out into the greying dusk and listened to their conversation. But she hardly heard them. Her eyes had filled with tears and her heart felt heavy. Her beloved always seemed so distant when she saw him together with other men. And yet there he was, not three steps away.

She heard her father's voice:

'Have you been to the Exhibition, Freutiger?'

It was 1897, the summer of the Great Exhibition.

'Yes, I did look in yesterday, since I was in town. And, as is my habit, you know – I've seen at least a hundred colossal world exhibitions – I asked as soon as I came in: Where is the belly dancer? And, you know? They didn't have a belly dancer! I almost fainted. So I took a look at the art. By the way, are you showing anything there?'

'Heavens, no. I never exhibit, but I sell anyway. I did go to see it last week and there certainly was stuff worth looking at. There was a Dane who had painted a sun that you couldn't look at without hurting your eyes. Pretty good! But God knows how they come up with all those modern tricks. Besides, I'm too old. Skoal, Lovén! You're not drinking, Stjärnblom, Skoal! There was a time in the eighties when I thought I was getting old-fashioned and decided to try to keep up with the times. Sunshine was out of style and people were getting tired of my pines, so I produced a *Row of Outhouses in Cloudy Weather*. I tried to get it into Furstenburg's or the Gothenburg Museum, but can you imagine? It got into the National Museum, where it's hanging to this day. That reassured me and I went back to my pines!'

'Skoal, old man,' Freutiger said. 'You and I, we've seen to the bottom of it all. Lovén, he can only look upward, since he's a tenor, and Stjärnblom is too young. Young people see nothing but themselves. We're just part of the background to them. Isn't that right, Arvid?

Lydia jumped when she heard his name. Arvid...how can anyone else address him that way?

'Skoal!' Stjärnblom answered.

'Pull yourself together, my boy,' the baron continued. 'Are you sitting there longing for your mountains in Värmland?'

'There are no mountains to speak of there,' Stjärnblom said.

'Well, how am I supposed to know that?' Freutiger said. 'I've been everywhere except around Sweden. As far as Värmland is concerned, my only connection is that my grandmother was in love with Geijer when she was young. He went skating with her on some lake there – isn't there a lake called Fryken? Yes, that's it, they went skating on Lake Fryken – some time at the beginning of the century. I guess it must have been 1813, because that was a cold winter. Anyway, my grandmother fell and landed on her rear end and Geijer got to see her legs, and they were much plumper and sturdier than he had ever expected them to be. And that was the end of that romance! But my grandfather, who owned a factory and was a practical sort of man and not the sort to babble about aesthetics, took her instead. That's the reason my name is Freutiger, why I exist at all and can sit here enjoying the beauties of nature.'

For some time, Lovén had shown signs of agitation. He coughed and cleared his throat, then suddenly stood up and began to sing an aria from Mignon. His beautiful voice rang out into the night a little more softly than usual: 'Never maiden dreamed – pure as an op'ning flower – That love so innocent as dwelt within her breast might e'er awake…to far more ardent power…'

Lydia, who had walked down to the sandy path beneath the veranda, was picking leaves from a barberry bush and crushing them between her fingers. Arvid Stjärnblom had raised himself and was now standing at the veranda railing where she had just stood. Slowly, Lydia walked down the path. It was already dark between the hedges. She stopped at the entrance of the lilac arbour. She heard Lovén's voice: 'Come, Oh Spring…and my dear ha-heart…'

His voice had cracked, of course, on the high B-flat.

She heard steps in the sand.

She recognized those steps. She knew very well whose they were. She hid in the arbour.

She heard a low voice:

'Lydia…?'

'Meow!' she answered from inside the arbour.

She was sorry right away and thought it was stupid of her to have meowed like a cat. She couldn't understand why she had done it. She stretched her arms toward him: 'Arvid – Arvid…'

They met in a long kiss.

And when they had to stop, he said in a low voice:

'Do you care for me just a little?'

She hid her face against his chest and didn't answer.

After a while she said:

'Do you see that star?'

'Yes.'

'Is that the evening star?'

'No, it can't be. The evening star goes down with the sun at this time of the year. Most likely it's a star called Capella.'

'Capella! What a beautiful name.'

'Yes, it is beautiful, but it only means "the Goat". Why that star is called the Goat, I really don't know. Actually, I really don't know anything.'

They stood silently. They heard the cry of the corncrake from far away.

He said:

'Why do you care for me?'

Again she hid her face against his chest and didn't answer.

'Don't you think Lovén sang beautifully just now?' he asked.

'Oh, yes,' she answered. 'He does have a beautiful voice.'

'And isn't Freutiger funny?'

'I suppose so. He's fun to listen to. And besides, he's not a bad person.'

'No, on the contrary…'

They stood close together, swaying back and forth and looking up at the stars.

Then he said:

'But it's because of you that his voice cracks when his feelings get the better of him and it's for your sake as well that Freutiger sits there and tells his lies. They are – both of them – in love with you. Now you know. So you can choose.'

He laughed a little. She kissed his forehead, then whispered, as though to herself:

'Who knows what's inside there...'

'Not anything very remarkable,' he answered. 'And it isn't always good to know...'

Looking deeply into his eyes, she answered:

'I believe in you, and that's enough for me. Just the fact that you are going to be in Stockholm this winter so that we can meet from time to time is enough for me. Is it at North Latin School that you are going to do your practice teaching?'

'Yes,' he answered, 'I suppose I will. I'm not planning to be a teacher, of course. That's really too hopeless a job. But since I have my bachelor's degree now, I might as well do the practice teaching. Then I suppose I'll work as a substitute for a while – while I'm waiting.'

'Waiting...? Waiting for what?'

'Oh, I don't know. Maybe for nothing at all. For a chance to do something worthwhile – whatever that might be... No, I really don't want to be a teacher. I can't possibly think of it as the future – not my future at any rate.

'Yes...' she said. 'The future – who knows what it will bring...?'

For a long time they stood in silence under the silent stars. Then she thought about something she had heard him say on the veranda, and said:

'I always thought there were high mountains in your Värmland. Is it really true that there aren't any?'

'Quite true,' he said. 'They may be higher than those here, but we don't have any real mountains. And I don't like mountains – that is, I like to climb them, but I don't like to live shut in by them. People talk about mountain landscapes, but I think they should be called valley landscapes. You live down in the valleys, not on the tops of the mountains. And the mountains get in the way of the sun the same as houses do in narrow alleys. As a result, it's ice-cold dusk almost the whole of the afternoon where I come from. There's only a short time, in the middle of the day, that is really beautiful there: when the sun is at its highest, or a little earlier even, over the plain of the Klara River. There's a wonderful light over all that beautiful countryside. You can look south where the sun shines over the wide valley and think: There, over there, that's where the world begins.'

Lydia was only half listening to him. She heard the word 'sun' and 'that's where the world begins' and she heard the cry of the corncrake in the field.

'Yes,' she said, 'the world... Do you think, Arvid, that you and I could some day make a little world for ourselves?'

He answered, also lost in thought:

'I suppose we could try.'

Suddenly there was the baron's voice from the veranda:

'Come on, boys, time to sing again! Let's have another drink!'

She wrapped her arms around his neck and whispered into his ear:

'I believe in you. I believe in you. And I can wait.'

Then there was Freutiger's voice again:

'Come on, boys!'

They hurried back to the veranda by different paths.

Later, Lydia stood at her open window looking out into the summer night. There were tears in her eyes. In the moonlight she could see the little boat in the bay, taking away the singers. They had stopped rowing. They were singing a serenade in her honour. They were singing: 'Why Are You So Far Away'. Notary Lovén's tenor rang out beautifully in the quiet night. The baron sang both first and second bass at the same time, at least that's what he thought, and the middle voice was that of her beloved.

Why are you so far away,
Oh, my love!
Softly shines the star,
Oh, my love!
The moon is ready to recline
from his quiet dance in time.
Good night my sweet love,
Good night my love.

Lydia sank down in a chair and sobbed with joy and fatigue. Suddenly she took down from its place on the wall under her mirror a small, old-fashioned flower holder made of gold-plated silver, with a turquoise-blue porcelain handle. She covered it with kisses and tears. It had been her mother's – it had held her mother's wedding bouquet.

The singing was over, they were rowing again and the boat was gliding away. Lovén and Stjärnblom rowed and Freutiger steered. Whether it was because they were all in love with the same girl, or for some other reason, no one said a word.

Sitting at the helm, the baron looked sombre. He was wondering about what he had said. Had he proposed or hadn't he? Well, he hadn't proposed to her directly. He had only vaguely hinted that she was his first real love. He had sat alone with old man Stille for a while at the end, and he must have said something more definite, because he remembered distinctly that the old man had answered: 'You and Lydia? Marry? How dare you, you old swine!'

Lovén, the customs officer, was rowing with the right oar and looking up at the stars. He remembered all the songs he had sung during the course of the evening, and he was sure that he had sung in such a way that anyone's heart must melt. True, his voice had cracked a couple of times. But still – but still, he really felt that he had reason to hope for the best.

Arvid Stjärnblom, the graduate, was rowing with his eyes closed. He was thinking about something that Lydia had said when they were in the arbour. 'I believe in you.' My God, that was really good! Very wonderful and good – that is – if she'd only stopped there… But then she'd said: 'I can wait.' And that was not good. It wasn't good at all. I can't bear the idea of someone waiting for me. Of someone expecting something from me. If I have something like that hanging over me all of the time, well then – I'll never amount to anything at all…

And besides, he continued, I am twenty-two years old. This is the beginning of my life. This is no time to tie myself down – not for life! No, you've got to be careful. You simply have to live first.

Nevertheless, at the same time, a warm wave flooded his whole being when he thought of her kisses. And then it occurred to him to wonder whether she was still a virgin.

Those were Arvid Stjärnblom's thoughts as he sat, sullen and worried, with his eyes closed, rowing with the left oar across the still black waters which reflected the stars and the tops of the pines.

It was a still, grey day at the beginning of October.

Arvid Stjärnblom was walking along a path in Djurgården. The path, bordered by elms with dark, leaning trunks, is the one that runs along the silent bay of Djugårdsbrunn beneath the rugged Skansen rocks. He had just passed the grounds where the Exhibition had been.

The Exhibition had closed a few days ago. He stopped for a moment and looked back. The makeshift walls from the reconstruction of sixteenth-century Stockholm had already been stripped bare by the wind and the rain, and the summer's gaudy market town grew more forlorn each day. The Hall of Industry's colourful dome, with its four minarets, still towered over it all and at the westernmost point the sun was just breaking through an opening in the clouds. It hung low in the sky, at the very edge of the haze that covered the city, and gleamed with a light that resembled old mellowed silver with the gold plating half worn off.

Arvid Stjärnblom gave the sun, the city and the Exhibition a long look of fond farewell and walked on.

He had recently begun his year of practice teaching at North Latin, and his subjects were Swedish, history and geography. Almost at the same time, through a distant relative named Markel, he had secured a job as proofreader at a big daily newspaper. But he wasn't thinking about those things now. He was thinking about Lydia.

There was never a day, not even an hour, when she wasn't in his thoughts. Often he thought: this must be love; it can't be anything else... He had decided not to get in touch with her in Stockholm, he wanted to let it happen by chance. Besides, they hadn't made any commitments that last evening on Runmar island – but then, they hadn't really known it would be their last meeting that summer... Still, he didn't feel that he could pay her a visit at home. Old man Stille thought of him as no more than a summer acquaintance, and they'd be surprised if he suddenly turned up at their little studio apartment in South Stockholm. They would realize that there was 'something' between Lydia and him. Neither Philip nor Otto nor the old man would imagine for one moment that he had come for their sake...

No...

A squirrel, its coat already shaggy and grizzled, suddenly hopped across the path, sat down and looked at him with curiosity and a sort of shyness that seemed calculatingly coy. Arvid stopped and looked into the small animal's pearly black eyes. That must have frightened him, for in a twinkling he disappeared, spiralling as quick as lightning up a tree.

Arvid had followed the path that went by way of Sirishov to Rosendal and then taken off to the right. There the path branched into many others and he chose one at random.

No, really, he couldn't pay her a visit. Perhaps he should write to her to ask for a meeting somewhere, for example here in Djurgården. She couldn't really be offended – after all that kissing last summer...but still...

It went against his grain to write and ask her for something when he himself had nothing to offer. After all, he hadn't achieved anything as yet – not anything at all.

Arvid Stjärnblom was not without pride; the trouble was he had no self-confidence. He certainly didn't think of himself as a failure, but he didn't believe himself capable of realizing his potential in the relatively near future. And the worst thing was that he didn't really dare rely on his feelings. He had been in love before, several times, for that matter, and had managed to get over it...

No, it was best to bide one's time – to keep hoping...

He stopped and drew lines on the dusty path with his cane.

Besides, what would come of it – what could possibly come of it? Marriage, after all, was out of the question. And 'seducing' her?

The very idea was unthinkable. Because if he were successful he would lose all respect for her, and if he weren't, well, then he'd lose every bit of respect for himself.

But...but oh my God, I do long for her so much! Just to meet her some time – just to see her some time...

Well, actually, he had seen her one time that autumn. It was the evening of the King's Silver Jubilee, with lights, fireworks and such crowds that you could hardly move. He had been standing on the corner of Nybroplan and Birgerjarlsgatan, when the cortège drove by with Europe's most handsome King, a man of almost seventy, standing in his carriage like a Roman conqueror. At that moment, a dim-witted old restaurateur, overwhelmed by a fear of anarchists, shouted: 'They're going to kill the King, they're going to kill the King!'...and, immediately afterwards, he had seen Lydia's face only a few steps away. But he was caught in the crowd and couldn't even raise his arm to greet her. All he was able to do was nod his head – and with his hat on at that! Thinking about it made him blush even now. But she had seen him and had inclined her head in answer. Then the crowd had driven them in opposite directions.

And all evening long, hour after hour, he had drifted randomly through the streets in the hope that he would see her again... Standing on the Strömgatan quay he had seen small black silhouettes moving about on the roof of the palace wing facing Strömmen. They were the King and his royal guests, there to watch the fireworks. Then suddenly there had been a commotion in the crowd around him, and he had heard someone say that the King was singing. 'It is an aria from *Robert*', someone else had said. And it had seemed to Arvid that there really was something like harp music in the air.

But he hadn't seen Lydia again.

It is strange that I never see her, he thought. Especially since I spend all my free time roaming the streets and avenues where I might possibly meet her.

He really did walk up and down Västerlånggatan two or three times almost every day. She lived in South Stockholm, and it was reasonable to suppose that she must sometimes have errands in the northern part of the city. And to get there she would almost certainly have to walk along Västerlånggatan. Sometimes he tried Stora Nygatan or Skeppsbron. But on those days she probably walked along Västerlånggatan, he decided.

It was quite unusual, therefore, for him to be walking around in Djurgården, as he was now.

He had sat down on a bench.

It was still light, where he was sitting. No large trees nearby, so it was bright enough to read if one wanted to.

He suddenly remembered that he had a couple of small books in his coat pocket. He had acquired them for a definite reason, and so he had to read them. One evening, when he was together with some friends, also substitute teachers and others doing their year of practice teaching, the conversation had turned to the teaching of religion. They had pretty much agreed that the practice of using Christianity as a basis for teaching morality was questionable, since this basis became shaky and fell apart for most students before they even finished school. They had wanted to make changes but were unable to agree on a solution. Someone had mentioned the existence of books that dealt with morality but were neutral in regard to religion, which were already being used by public schools in France. Arvid had become interested, decided to order them, and today they had arrived. These were the books that were in his coat pocket.

But what had he wanted them for? He hardly knew. He wasn't especially attracted to writing a 'textbook on morality'. The title alone was enough to make the whole book seem ridiculous. But still...it somehow seemed to him that this was a problem that he could solve...a project he could work on...a blank he could fill in... How to go about it, he didn't have the slightest idea, nor, for that matter, whether he would be the right person to do it.

He took the books out of his pocket.

By the looks of the covers, one of them was for the primary grades and the other for a higher level. He started reading the primary book, *Manuel d'Education Morale*, by A. Burdeau, Président de la Chambre des Députés.

Arvid was amazed. President of the Chamber of Deputies! The third most important person in France! More important even than the President of the Assembly! That a man like that sits himself down to write a book for little school children was not only impressive, it was downright touching.

He continued to read:

'My children, from the teaching of morals we can learn how we should behave at present and in the future in order to become honourable human beings and good Frenchmen, just like those who have lived before us.'

'...like those who have lived before us'? Hmm!

Arvid read on:

'What is it that constitutes the greatest misfortune of the ignorant? The greatest misfortune of the ignorant lies in the fact that he does not understand the extent to which his condition is unfortunate.'

What?

'What is it that makes learning of value? Learning is of value because it makes becoming honourable human beings easier for us. Is there anything as important for a human being as food and clothing? Yes, there is something that is just as necessary as food and clothing: it is a moral education.'

Arvid's head was reeling. What complete nonsense! Was it possible that Mr A. Burdeau, President of the Chamber of

Deputies and the third most important man in the whole of France was joking? Was it really possible to teach French school boys that sort of thing? It would certainly be impossible here... No, really – reading this was a waste of time. Maybe he was a worthy President, but this – he obviously didn't have the slightest idea how this sort of a book should be written...but then neither do I, for that matter...

Absentmindedly, he continued leafing through the book, and read such information as the fact that a teacher was a civil servant (in bold type) and that he represented the state, and there were recommendations about hygiene, there was some criticism of Napoleon III and the Second Empire, and so on and so forth.

Then, on the last page:

1. Who are the human beings we love naturally? First of all our parents, and then those whom we know and who have been good to us.
2. Whom do we love without knowing them? We love our fellow countrymen without knowing them.
3. Whom should we love furthermore? Furthermore, we should love all human beings, even those who are not Frenchmen.
4. Can we love the Germans? We cannot possibly love those who have injured France and who oppress Frenchmen in Alsace-Lorraine.
5. What should we do about the above situation? We must tear away from the Germans our brothers whom they have robbed from us.
6. Should we then, after freeing Alsace-Lorraine, do unto the Germans the evil they have done to us? Certainly not; that would be unworthy of us as Frenchmen.
7. What are the nations in relation to each other? In relation to each other, nations are equal.
8. What is the relationship between nations and mankind? Just as citizens are part of a nation, so are nations part of mankind.

9. What constitutes the honour of France? The fact that France has always considered what is best for all nations constitutes the honour of France.

And then, at the very end:

'Vive l'Humanité! Vive la France!'

Thoughts were racing through Arvid's mind.

No, Mr Bourdeau, that is the wrong way, that much I know. You might as well keep to the old catechism. But beyond that I've no idea what to do either.

A little distance away, at a bend in the path, he saw, in the pale light of a sunbeam, two figures walking towards him. Despite the distance, he was immediately able to see that they were a young girl and an older man.

'If only it were Lydia and her father,' flew through his head…

His heart was pounding and he felt himself blushing. Instinctively, he held the book up to hide his face, but he could not keep from peeping over its edge.

It took only a second for him to see that it was Lydia. But she wasn't walking with her father. It was another man who appeared to be in his early fifties. He had a short, grizzled beard and generally looked what people would call distinguished.

Arvid got up and greeted them. Lydia inclined her head deeply, but without meeting his eyes. The older gentleman returned his greeting as well.

He watched them disappear around the next bend. Glancing absentmindedly at the book still in his hand, he noticed that he was holding it upside down.

Arvid had now taken out the other book, the one for older children, and he leafed through it at random.

'Moral law is the same for everyone, regardless of climate, age, sex, intelligence: all human beings are aware of its significance. Moral law is universal and very clear. Its message can be summarized in few words: do good and not evil. The whole world understands these words, because from deep inside the voice of our conscience tells us: this is good and that is evil'.

Arvid put the book back into his pocket, together with the other one, and walked towards town. It was beginning to get dark.

He stood still for a moment: he had forgotten to check the author's name. He took the book out again, and read: Léopold Mabilleau, *docteur ès Lettres, directeur du Musée social*.

I really wonder, he thought, whether Mr Léopold Mabilleau is in his right mind...

★

Arvid Stjärnblom had rented a furnished room on Dalagatan. It was small and the furniture was shabby, but it had a large open view to the west, over Sabbatsberg, all the way to the granite cliffs of Kungsholmen, which marked the city limits.

After a hurried dinner alone at the restaurant he went home to his lonely room.

He lit the lamp but did not draw the curtain. It was cold in the room, and, as he did every evening, he lit the firewood that the landlady placed in the tiled stove in the morning. At about nine o'clock he would leave for his job at the newspaper.

He began to cut the pages of a newly published book – it was Strindberg's *Inferno*. Then he stopped and began to play absentmindedly with the paperknife.

Who on earth could that old man have been?

Maybe some old friend of the family's, someone she would call 'Uncle' and who had met her by chance and then forced his company upon her without asking permission...

Yes, most likely, that's the way it was...most likely.

But really, he remembered now...he had felt so very strange.

He tried to forget about it, to think of something else.

Suddenly he began to think about his name. 'Arvid Stjärnblom'.

He hated his name. He didn't like his Christian name because it was the same as that of the country's most famous tenor, and men were generally contemptuous of the character of tenors. And his family name: 'Stjärnblom'! So typical of the most common middle class family names formed by combining the names of two objects in nature – usually ones that are as unrelated as possible. For example 'Nordkvist' – what on earth did a point of the compass have to do with a twig? Or 'Söderlund'. Of course, you could imagine a grove of trees somewhere in the south, but, if you should happen to be south of it, you would have to call it 'Nordlund'! As far as Stjärnblom is concerned – a star and a flower together is really too much of a good thing, damn it!

But...that distinguished older man, who could he possibly have been?

Anyway, his father, the old forest ranger back in Värmland, had had that name for more than sixty years without ever thinking that there was anything ridiculous about it. And his father's father and grandfather before him. So, I guess I will have to put up with it as well. Since, after all, 'I am no better than my fathers'.

But his great-great-grandfather's name had not been Stjärnblom. It had been Andersson. And that, at the time, was not a family name at all. It simply meant that he was the son of someone called Anders.

And so all I know about my background is that my grandfather's grandfather was the son of someone called Anders. There are, I suppose, many who don't even know that much about their origins!

The word *hidalgo* suddenly entered his mind. It was a title given to Spanish nobility of low rank, and meant 'son of someone'.

True, he decided, it all depends upon where you are. At home I am the son of someone: although not rich, my father is a well-known and respected member of the community. Here, however, I am nothing at all. Here, at best, my son can become an *hidalgo*: that is, if I should have a son...which I most likely won't. By the time I get to the point where I have the right to put children into the world, I will be so old and decrepit that I'll no longer be able to justify doing it...

But who was that distinguished-looking old man...?

For a moment Arvid thought that he had seen him before on some newspaper photograph, but he still didn't know who he was.

He was pacing back and forth in his room. Two, three steps at a time – that's all the space there was.

He stopped in front of the map of northern Värmland hanging over the sofa. The first thing he had done after moving into the room was to take down all of the landlady's horrible paintings. He didn't have any of his own to hang up instead; while doing it he had smiled and thought that that was just typical – it's always easy to tear things down, but building them up again, that was another story. Even with the best of intentions he could never produce a painting, not even of the sort comparable to the trash he had taken down. Still, that didn't mean he had to live with the wretched stuff! So he had put up his map of Värmland for want of something better.

Besides, where the paintings had been the brownish-rose wallpaper from some forgotten part of the eighties could now speak for itself. Anyway, why should he care about the looks of a room he would occupy only for a short time?

He stood there staring at the map. He read the names of the towns, estates and mountains he had cherished and knew so well...Stöllet, Dalby, Ransby, Gunneby, Långav, Likenäs, Transtrand, Branäsberget, Femtåberget...

Femtåberget. He remembered that mountain so well. Like a

large, blue shadow, it stood straight to the south of his childhood home. It could hardly be called a mountain when compared, for example, to a mountain in Peru called Chimborazo. But Femtåberget happened to be the highest in that area, and so it was referred to as a mountain. Looked at from the north, it had an architectural beauty, good proportions and seemed to have a well-designed contour with three peaks, the highest in the middle. Whenever he had been home on vacation from high school in Karlstad, he had referred to the three peaks as: Progressus, Culmen, Regressus. Upward, Highest, Downward! But he couldn't understand why it had been it been called Femtåberget. Did it, perhaps, seen from some other place, resemble a foot with five toes? Not at all. Maybe its name had come from the little stream that flowed down its western slope into the Klara river? You don't name a mountain after a stream that happens to originate from some spring on its slope. The contrary would be more likely. A name, it seems, can mean so much – and so little...

For example Lydia Stille. Such a beautiful-sounding name. Lydia Stille, Lydia Sti–

The doorbell rang. He listened... No one went to answer it. Apparently the landlady wasn't home.

He didn't feel like opening it. If it's important, he reasoned, they'll ring again.

Seconds passed, perhaps a minute even, but it didn't ring again. So he went out to look.

No one there. And nothing in the mailbox.

He sat down again in front of his fire and stirred the embers. The fire had almost burned down. He thought about things from long ago – his last year of high school in Karlstad. And he remembered Mrs Kravatt, the lady who during that winter and the following spring, just before graduation, had introduced him to the great mystery...

Mrs Kravatt had been a little over thirty, the widow of a

janitor, and the best cook in town. She even cooked dinner at the governor's on special occasions. In her private life, however, she wasn't much interested in food. Instead she was very much given to lovemaking. He used to go and visit her on Sunday mornings, and often rushed over to her place during lunchtime. He wasn't the only recipient of her favours. He shared them with five or six of his friends. Whenever he brought up the fact that this was distressing to him, she answered simply and without affectation: 'What's good is good, and I'm only human!'

However, she was interested in poetry as well, and sometimes burst into tears when he recited something from Victor Rydberg or Fröding for her in bed.

She also had to be paid, but that was mostly for the sake of form and decency. The fee for high school students was two crowns, and credit was easily available whenever cash was a problem. She simply did what was good for its own sake, which is generally regarded as the most moral attitude to which a human being can aspire.

He thought of her now with unreserved gratitude and blushed when he remembered that he still owed her forty-two crowns. In vain, he tried to find moral support in the knowledge that at least three of his classmates had left town owing just about as much.

Suddenly he thought about Mr Léopold Mabilleau again, and his moral education for older students. 'The voice of our conscience tells us what is good.' Well, that certainly makes Mr Mabilleau just as superfluous as his book! Mrs Kravatt knew what was good without the benefit of his writings! She simply obeyed her 'voice of conscience'.

Arvid paced back and forth in his room. Two, three steps towards the window, two, three steps back to the tiled stove.

He stopped again in front of the map over the sofa. The map

of northern Värmland. The place where he was born: the place where he had lived most of his life. Now he was here, in a shabby little furnished room with brownish-rose wallpaper, in the country's capital. Where would he end up? He remembered the big river he had known in his childhood, the river with the three names – one name in Norway, where it flows like a wild mountain brook from a mountain lake; another in Värmland, where it widens and slows down so that it can be navigated by steam boats for a distance of seventy to eighty kilometres before it swells to become a large lake, and finally it changes to its third name as Sweden's largest river, and finds its way to the sea, the Atlantic ocean and the world.

He remembered a poem he had once written in the spring before he graduated and which had been printed in the Karlstadstidning under a pen name. How jubilant he had been when he had seen it in print! He remembered that in his happiness he had walked ten kilometres along Klara Älven, all the way to Lunden, and that he had sat there for hours on a rock looking out across the large, blue lake… Then, back in Karlstad, he had, of course, not been able to resist going to see Mrs Kravatt. He had read the poem to her and had received a poet's reward…

He found the poem now in a desk drawer. The newspaper clipping had already turned yellow:

I WENT WALKING WITH MY MOTHER
I went walking with my mother
one summer day in a land of dreams
with blue mountains and quiet shining streams
and she held my hand.
Our path descended gently
towards the lush green dale.
At the end lay the mirror of the river.
On it, a hundred sun-warmed sails

and ships both white and grey
were gliding in a dream-like silence.
In the river was an island,
on the island lay a town
with red roofs, their ridges in a broken row
around which light and shadows vied.
Beyond the town the view was wrapped
in haze and mist. There was the sea.
Mother, I asked, please say,
will this road ever take us all the way
down to the shore?
I want to go down to the sea
and sail until I can be
in the blue lands.

Very gently mother answered:
Be patient, child, soon you will be grown;
then you can go to the seas
and sail, so your mother believes,
away to the far blue lands.
Be patient now and restrain your blood,
then on this stream, your own white ship will come,
your life's bright ship of luck
to take you out into the world.
Steer then, with a firm hand,
and all will go well on your voyage!
First you will reach the city
where on both towers and peaks there is light.
You don't know, my child, how dark it is to live inside.
Yet you will live there for a time,
you know not how long or short;
and you will both struggle and strive,
until your bright ship of luck comes to its port.
In the tower the bells will ring without a doubt

when your ship puts out
and leaves and takes you far away
from the town where in the dark and close
your fate lay buried.
It takes you out to sea.
But beyond the sea there is another shore,
and there lies the blue land of your dreams,
and there, there you will always be.
That is what your mother believes.

*

So was my mother's belief
That was long ago, I have forgotten
where that land was, its mountains and blue rivers.
And it has been a long time since I last saw my mother.
Perhaps it was a dream.

'And it has been a long time since I last saw my mother.' Yes, that was very true. He had only been six years old when she died.

This poem was almost the only thing he had ever written. The only thing he had finished, at any rate.

No – he wasn't a poet. He looked at the world with eyes that were too sober, too unimaginative. He didn't have the happy and necessary capacity for dreaming, for becoming intoxicated by his dreams. Nor, perhaps, was he irresponsible enough to be a poet! Of course, a poet must have some sort of conscience, but it had to be of the most relaxed sort in existence.

No, he definitely didn't want to be a poet. That wasn't his ambition. No thanks!

Ambition…?

'Do I have any sort of ambition?'

He started pacing again. Two, three steps forward: two, three steps back. The room hardly allowed for much else. He stopped in front of the mirror over the washstand.

'What is my ambition?' he asked himself.

And it seemed as though the mirror answered:

'If you do have any sort of ambition, more than just to get through life tolerably well, then it is...'

He stared into the mirror with horror. No, he thought, no – he almost pleaded with the mirror: no, don't tell me...

And it seemed to him as though the mirror answered:

'Well, you've asked me, and I will answer you. If you have any ambition at all, then it is this: you need to make a name for yourself that will go down in the history of your people. Not the history of its literature or any subsidiary part thereof, but in the very history of your people.'

Apparently, I've lost my mind, Arvid decided. Therefore it is important to at least appear as though I haven't. It's almost nine o'clock, time to go to work.

He took his hat, his coat and his cane and left.

Autumn progressed. Dusk came early and wet pavements reflected splashes of light from gas lamps and lighted windows.

One evening, late in November, Arvid Stjärnblom arrived at the newspaper office. He felt somewhat uneasy. He had been to the Opera and now, for the first time, he had to write a review.

This was how it had happened:

At about four in the afternoon he had arrived at the office to receive his assignment for the evening. Markel, the assistant editor, wasn't there. While he was waiting, Arvid had leafed through the most recent issue of *Ord och Bild* and started whistling the adagio from Beethoven's *Pathétique*, which for some reason was going through his head. Suddenly, Dr Doncker, the editor-in-chief, walked in through the open door – he was almost never at the office at that hour. He was handsome and elegant – perhaps a little too handsome and a little too elegant for a man in his early forties.

'Was that you, Mr Stjärnblom, I heard whistling the *Pathétique*?' he asked in his nasal voice.

'Yes – please excuse me!'

'Oh, that's quite all right. As a matter of fact, it's perfect. You can go to the Opera tonight and write a review. There'll be this little girl making her debut as Marguerite in *Faust*. The regular music critic is sick, and I've been invited out to dinner. Goodbye!'

Whenever the regular critic was unavailable, the editor-in-chief would usually substitute. Until very recently, Dr Doncker had been a geology professor, but, as Markel used to say, he wrote Latin verse better than Swedish prose and was otherwise interested only in business and women. He was able to write tolerably well about almost anything – 'even about rare and unusual coins,' Markel had said...

Anyway, that was how it had happened. Now Arvid sat brooding over his typewriter.

He had quickly learned to use a typewriter. Of course, this didn't mean that he saved much time when he had to make up the text himself, but that was seldom the case. Usually his assignments at the editorial office consisted of translating political articles from German and English newspapers, which the 'minister of foreign affairs' in the office would give him, marked with blue crayon, and serial stories from *Le Journal*, which another colleague of higher standing gave him, marked in red. When he typed the translations, he accomplished in half an hour what otherwise would take him two or three.

Now, however, he was supposed to make up something by himself. He abandoned the typewriter and sat down at the desk.

Markel was ranting and raving next door:

'Hell and damnation! Goddamn it to hell! I can't take it any more!

The door opened suddenly and Markel came in, his face livid with rage.

'Can you believe it,' he said. 'The scoundrel gave me his word of honour that humbug of a pastor's article wouldn't go in...'

'What scoundrel and what humbug of a pastor?'

'What scoundrel, you ask? Doncker, of course! And the pastor is one of the worst kind of humbugs: a "liberal" who sent in an article that, freely interpreted, implies that belief in the Bible, church dogma or anything else for that matter is completely unnecessary for a pastor in the Swedish church, and that we absolutely need more pastors and bishops. There are too few bishops! We've only got twelve or thirteen and should have at least fourteen or fifteen of them! Right now, our man is too young and insignificant to be considered for a bishopric, but you can be sure he's looking out for his future! Well, I happened to see the proofs and went to see Doncker. He took a look at them and said that he'd never seen the article, nor had he ever heard about it. That's quite possible...'

'But,' Arvid interrupted, 'how can an article go to the compositors and be typeset without either the editor-in-chief or the assistant editor knowing anything about it?'

'How, you ask? And you've been here for more than two months! The dumbwaiter, of course, you little fool! The dumbwaiter out there in the corridor, which constantly takes manuscripts down to the compositors and comes up again with proofs! Anyone can come in from the street, and, if there is no one in the corridor, he can just send a manuscript down on it. Or, if he doesn't happen to know his way around, he just has to find one of our underlings – you, for example! – and ask him to do it. And if a manuscript goes down to the compositors it also gets set! And then it goes into the paper, if I don't happen to catch it first! Well, I had Doncker's word of honour that this rubbish was going into the waste paper basket. Now I've just found a new proof of the article – a proof that had been read and edited! So I called the foreman and was informed that Doncker had telephoned him an hour or two ago and told him that the article must definitely be included! The scoundrel's been out having dinner, and he's met the pastor or some other semi-religious trash who's changed his mind, and the result is that the article will be in tomorrow's paper! Or rather, it won't be in tomorrow's paper, since my being in charge today means I have the right to postpone longer articles if they are not of current interest. However, it will go in the day after tomorrow, when I'm not in charge! Hell! But show me, what's that you've written? Doncker told me that he'd sent you to the Opera...'

He picked up Arvid's manuscript, looked at it absentmindedly and went on:

'Today's clergy seem to have forgotten their age-old purpose.

You can find out about it in the writings of the prophet Malachi: "The mouth of the pastor shall safeguard the truth." Notice that he said safeguard. He didn't say "disseminate". To be a pastor and disseminate the truth at the same time, that is impossible. To do both at the same time! How can that be possible?'

He stopped talking and began to read.

Suddenly he brightened.

'Why, this is really good!' he said. 'You know, I have to check it, since I found you this job without knowing anything at all about you – only that you're a distant relation. So I'm sort of responsible for what you write, you see. But this is really good! "Miss Klarholm's voice and singing talent point to almost boundless possibilities…etc. Her acting, however, displays a lack of instruction. Marguerite is not supposed to go mad until the prison scene, but Miss Klarholm acts crazy almost from the beginning. Her Marguerite seems to have been born mad."

'That's good,' Markel said. 'Of course, I have no idea about how she really acted, but people don't like it when others are praised too much. Those whom the praise is intended for are never satisfied anyway, and the others are jealous. But if a critic tells off only one comedian or singer, then only one person is upset, and all the others are happy! So, just tell her off! It's absolutely right to try spreading a little happiness around.'

Markel left, but came back immediately:

'By the way,' he said, 'old man Stille is dead…'

'What…what did you say?'

Markel was surprised:

'What do you mean? How does it affect you? He was old, and all of us have to die some time. "Almost all", as Louis XIV's court preacher added quickly when he saw the King's face darkening…'

'Oh, nothing,' Arvid said, 'but I didn't know he'd been ill. After all, I only knew him slightly.'

'Well, he wasn't ill. It was a simple streetcar accident.'

'What happened?'

'Oh, my God – he'd been sitting in a tavern at Norrmalmstorg, having a bottle of wine with some other old fellows. Then he was going to take the streetcar home. One of those horse-drawn cars we still have in Stockholm in this year of our Lord 1897. Anyway, the horses were trotting along nicely, and old man Stille, somewhat affected by the wine, forgot that he was over sixty and tried to jump up into the car. He stumbled and fell and hit his head on the pavement. That was a couple of hours ago, and the rest of the story is as you'd expect – an ambulance, then Serafimer Hospital – and at around ten o'clock they called to say he was dead. The obituary has been written – we used information from the *Nordisk Familjebok*. It's been typeset and proofread. Here's a copy. Since you knew him a little, maybe you could add a few lines of a more personal nature. That is, if you feel like it.

Markel left.

Arvid sat with the damp proofs in his hand:

An unfortunate accident – Anders Stille, the well-known and highly esteemed landscape painter... Born 1834... Student at the Academy of Arts in the 1850s... Medal in Paris 1868... *Island Pines after the Rain* in the Galleries du Luxembourg... *Row of Outhouses in Cloudy Weather* in the National Museum in Stockholm... Unacquainted with the newer trends in art... Somewhat in the background during recent years... A modest and upright artist, a respected and much-loved man... A widower for the past few years... Mourned by two sons and a daughter...

Arvid sat and stared into space, preoccupied and absentminded at the same time...

No, there wasn't anything he could add. Instead, he would have liked to take a blue crayon and cross out that part about 'somewhat in the background', but he didn't have the right to change anything in someone else's article. Still, it did bother him. Perhaps Lydia would think that he had been the one who had written it.

Lydia...

He jumped up all of a sudden, locked the door to the editorial office and burst into violent sobs.

After a while he stamped his foot. What on earth am I doing? Twenty-three years old in a few weeks and I sit here crying like a baby...completely ridiculous. He rushed into the bathroom, splashed water on his face and wiped away all traces of tears. Then he returned to the office and unlocked the door.

He should be able to go home now. It was a little after one a.m. and he had nothing more to do. Because of his assignment as temporary music critic, he had been excused from proofreading that night.

But he did want to see a proof of his review before leaving. He remembered something he had written about the young debutante: '...her Marguerite seems to have been born mad...' He thought he'd cross that out. She did have a beautiful voice: that, at least, had been a success. It would be a shame to poison her happiness by being unnecessarily nasty.

He phoned down to the compositors to ask whether the review had already been typeset. They said it had. He asked for the proofs.

Markel yanked the door open:

'You finished yet? Come on in and have a drink!'

'Thanks,' Arvid answered, 'I'm just waiting for my proofs.'

'Oh, don't worry. Old Johansson's down there, and he's completely reliable. Besides, it's impossible to misinterpret your handwriting.'

But I wanted to change something...'

'There's nothing for you to change. I've read it and it was perfectly all right! Besides,' he added, 'I'm going to see to it that you won't have to proofread any more night after night. Not that you don't do a good job – quite the opposite, as a matter of fact. I was almost worried when I saw how good you were – worried for your future! A young man who can proofread is usually unable to do anything else, and that means that he gets stuck doing it until his beard turns white. Like old man Johansson.'

It was dark in the main editorial office. No one was around. In the doorway to Markel's cubbyhole a light shone from a triangular, emerald-green lampshade.

Markel's room was situated between the editor-in-chief's room and the main editorial office.

A well dressed, very young man was sitting in a corner of the little sofa. He seemed to be half asleep.

'Allow me to introduce you,' Markel said. 'This is Mr Stjärnblom, a son of one of my fifty or sixty cousins – Mr Henrik Rissler, who has written an immoral novel, which, however, as far as I'm concerned, is no more immoral than any novel should be in order to be readable.'

They exchanged greetings. Then Markel continued, addressing himself to Arvid:

'Listen to this! Rissler is, as you know, one of our paper's occasional and unimportant literary contributors. This morning he came in with a contribution – a little short story – for twenty-five crowns. Unfortunately, the newspaper was as short of cash as the promising young writer himself. So Doncker had the bright idea of taking care of the problem by saying that he – can you believe this? – has to read the rubbish before paying for it! Since Rissler is a good-natured bastard, he didn't get angry. Instead, he turns up here in the middle of the night to find out whether Doncker has read the story and whether the cashier's is open!'

'My dear Markel,' Rissler broke in, 'you have a fabulous talent for talking nonsense. I've come here for the simple reason that it's too late to go to a bar. I was out to dinner and stayed too long. By the way, Doncker was there as well.'

'So you were at Rubin's...? Was that humbug of a pastor there too?'

'There was a humbug of a pastor there, but I don't know what his name was.'

Markel uttered a war cry:

'Ha! Do you recall what I said a little while ago, Arvid?'

Arvid nodded.

'Well,' mumbled Markel, 'the article won't be in tomorrow's edition at any rate. I took care of that. Skoal, boys!'

'Skoal. Anything new on the Dreyfus affair?'

'Not today. I suppose it must have been about a week ago that Mathieu Dreyfus accused Esterhazy of having written the list. According to the Paris newspapers it looks as though there's going to be another court-martial – for the sake of form. That's what you can read between the lines.'

'Strange business,' said Rissler. 'I've just been in Paris for a while – came home the day before yesterday. On the boulevards I heard the newsboys yelling: "Scheurer-Kestner's had a Negress for a lover!" As he's about seventy years old, Scheurer-Kestner has certainly had the time to find all sorts of things to amuse himself with. How that can be used as evidence of Dreyfus's guilt is pretty hard to understand, however.'

'Quiet! There's someone in the corridor...'

Markel held his breath and listened.

Then they heard muffled footsteps, followed by the squeaking of a door. Now steps again from the editor-in-chief's office. A key turned in the lock between the chief's and Markel's office. Arvid looked at his watch. It was a quarter past two.

'Sh-sh,' Markel whispered. 'He has a woman with him!'

They heard something rustle.

'Well then, Skoal,' Markel suddenly said in a very loud voice.

There was silence. Then they heard steps that no longer made an effort to be silent, going from the chief's office through the corridor to Markel's door. The door opened and Doncker stuck his head in.

'Good evening,' he said. 'Could I possibly ask you gentlemen to do me a completely private and personal favour?'

'What's on your mind?' Markel said. 'How about a little drink first?'

'No, thanks. I just wanted to ask whether this pleasant little get-together could be continued in another room – preferably somewhere at the other end of the building?'

'Why, of course,' Markel answered. 'But on one condition!'

'And what might that be?'

'That the pastor's article never gets into print! Never, that is!'

Dr Doncker snorted and gave a little half-smothered laugh:

'My dear Markel, why in hell do you think I care about that pastor's article? You can do what you damn well please with it.'

'Good. We have an agreement then. And remember, I've got two witnesses!'

Carrying their bottles and glasses, they moved in a silent procession down the corridor, in the dim light of a single bulb. Doncker stood in the doorway watching them disappear. Markel turned around and whispered loudly:

'I guess there's no point in asking whether you want to come along for a drink?'

'No thanks,' Doncker answered.

★

On the way home Arvid picked up a girl. That is to say, a girl picked him up.

There was lots of snow and it was already bitter cold during the first days of December that year. It was the same on the day old man Stille was buried.

Arvid had gone out to the New Cemetery to catch a glimpse of Lydia. He had sent a simple wreath for the coffin.

He took his place among a small group of people near the entrance of the chapel. He recognized some artists, mostly grey-haired men, and also the director of the Academy of Arts, with his aristocratic profile, the most highly regarded artist of his generation. There were some others who had come out of curiosity, but certainly not many.

He could see the funeral procession coming up the road, in step, the hearse with its silver decorations, a last poor remnant of the baroque taste for showy ornaments in life and death, shining in the pale December sun. The coffin was lifted from the carriage by big hands in white cotton gloves. The members of the cortege stepped out of the carriages and got in line. Lydia walked behind the coffin, looking young and slender, her head slightly inclined behind the veil. Beside her was Philip, pale, his nose pinched by the frost. Otto was not there – he was, of course, supposed to go to America...and had apparently left already.

Arvid had taken off his hat when the coffin passed and was still holding it when Lydia walked by. But her eyelids were lowered and she didn't see him. Behind her the few relations and closest friends, the director of the Academy of Arts followed by the grey-bearded artists entered the chapel and the doors were closed.

Arvid turned around and started towards town.

It reminded him of *The Lost Son* in the National Museum. The desolate snowy winter twilight over the graveyard was the same as that in the painting.

He stood still for a moment, next to a tall stone with a medallion in bronze on it. It said EMANUEL DONCKER in faded gold letters. The famous chemist had been the grandfather of the editor-in-chief. The profile on the medallion was actually reminiscent of his grandson's.

Arvid chuckled. He remembered that night at the editorial office a couple of days ago. He had opened the paper the following morning with more interest than usual, looking for old man Stille's obituary as well as his own review of the concert. But the first thing that met his eyes was the article by the pastor, which had been placed somewhere between the editorial and something else. Of course, afterwards he did also find what he was looking for. The obituary had been marred by a couple of stupid typos. He remembered having seen them and correcting them, but he had obviously forgotten to return the proofs by way of the dumbwaiter... And, as far as his review was concerned, 'Her Marguerite appears to have been born mad' looked even worse in print. He was shocked: could I really have written something so mean, so impertinent? Why I remember wanting to cross it out on the proof, but then something happened and I forgot all about it...

He walked slowly among the graves with his collar turned up.

He had to chuckle again. He remembered Markel's explanation when, having arrived at the editorial office, he had asked him how on earth the pastor's article had got in.

'There can only be one explanation,' Markel had said. 'For once I trusted him – after all I had two witnesses! And after that I sat and talked peacefully and unsuspectingly with you and Rissler. In the meantime, Doncker must have remembered that he had given the pastor a promise that was equally solemn! So, while his lady was busy unhooking her corset and loosening her drawers, he suddenly remembers that we don't have enough bishops! He phones the foreman: the article must go in! And in it went! After all, he is editor-in-chief. Besides, you can't really be angry with him. When I scolded him for his little dirty trick, he answered me: "My dear Markel, in the sort of situation I was in last night you make whatever promise is necessary!" And, for once, I agreed with him.'

A few minutes after his conversation with Markel, Arvid had met the chief in the corridor. He had stopped and said:

'I've read your little review, Mr Stjärnblom, and really, it was just right! "Born mad" – very good! I had already noticed that we could use you. After New Year you will get a regular salary, a hundred crowns a month to start with.'

Arvid continued to walk slowly towards town. At Norrtull he took a streetcar.

★

A few days after the funeral Arvid wrote a letter to Lydia. Among other things, he wrote:

You have not been out of my thoughts a single day since we were last together. I have kept myself from contacting you only because I thought I should, and had to. After all, I have nothing to offer you – nothing at all except a distant and uncertain future.

Her answer came the next day:

Arvid. Thanks for your letter. I have read it again and again, but don't understand it – yes, I do understand it, but still, I don't really understand it!

But some day I would like to meet you again. Not now – I am so tired and sad now. But some time soon.

Life is so empty now that father is dead.

Lydia

On January 11th, 1898 the military tribunal found Esterhazy not guilty. The honour of France and the French army was unable to bear the idea that a dirty and insignificant act of treason, for which a brilliant and wealthy staff officer, who happened to be Jewish, had been condemned, was, in reality, committed by an unimportant officer of foreign birth, a morally disreputable and degenerate lout. On January 13th Zola's 'J'accuse' was published in *L'Aurore* and a short summary of its contents was immediately telegraphed around the world. Two days later the issue of *L'Aurore* arrived at the editorial office of the *Nationalblad*

Markel was beaming. He surrounded himself with his editorial staff. Olof Levini, the poet, critic and literary historian came out of his room. He was already famous and controversial then. From another room came Torsten Hedman, playwright and theatre critic. Even the writer Henrik Rissler turned up – he had come to find out what was new in the Dreyfus Affair. And news he got! Markel took his scissors, cut the enormous article into pieces and distributed them left and right.

'You who can type,' he said to Arvid, 'you can take the first three columns, so that they can get started with them at the printers, and in the meantime I'll have time to number and put the rest in order.'

'But, Olle, please,' he said to Professor Levini, 'please try to write so that they can read it down there!'

Levini and Hedman, of course, didn't usually do translations, but this was a special occasion.

'Can't I have a piece to work on too?' Henrik Rissler said. 'I don't usually write without being paid for it, but I want to be a part of this!'

Rissler was well known for being lazy.

When Arvid was finished with his translation, he went to the proofreading room to help old Johansson with the reading. The first proofs had already come up. By two o'clock the whole colossal article had been translated, typeset and proofread, so that it could be included as an addition to the provincial edition and as a special edition in Stockholm.

Thanks to Markel, the *Nationalblad* had, from the beginning, taken the correct course over the Dreyfus affair. When it came to other matters, especially political questions, his opinions could be somewhat unsteady, like the nighttime rambling of a poet. As far as politics were concerned, the paper was more or less indifferent – its position was 'beyond the parties', according to the most recent subscription application. In this respect, as with so many others, the paper made a virtue out of a necessity. For historical reasons the paper could not consider a connection to any political party. The *Nationalblad* had been founded some time in the 1880s as an organ representing ultra-reactionary, protectionist and agrarian interests. It could never have managed independently, that is, without the financial backing from big industry. However, after the protectionist breakthrough at the end of the 1880s the interests the paper was supposed to defend achieved what they wanted and the patrons, satisfied and delighted, apparently were no longer willing to fill this 'sieve of the Danaïdes'. The paper went into a decline, and in early spring 1897 there was a crash! The last of the patrons, who for the past few years had been its only economic support, was forced to stop his payments and put his interests into receivership. Among his weakest active ones was his controlling shares in the *Nationalblad* – the creditors were leaning towards making them passive… But at that point something happened.

A financier by the name of Henry Steel, who wasn't at all interested in politics, but had strong cultural and artistic interests instead, had come into contact with a circle of poets and writers – the great poet P. A. von Gurkblad, Olof Levini, Torsten Hedman, Henrik Rissler and others – even Doncker was part of the group. He allowed them to inveigle him into promising his financial support to a new paper. It would be a liberal evening paper, because they all detested the *Aftonpost*. The plan was to drive the *Aftonpost* out of circulation. The new paper, as stated, would be liberal, or rather, radical, but with a somewhat stronger emphasis on national points of view than that of the current liberal party. For some secret reason Doncker was to be editor-in-chief. P. A. von Gurkblad was to support the paper as administrative director and as a voluntary contributor. Olof Levini was to be the literary critic and write editorials on cultural affairs. Torsten Hedman would write about theatre and art and whatever else he felt like. And so on. Markel – who was part of the group as well – was to deal with politics.

As fate would have it, at the time of the crash Henry Steel's bank – that is, Henry Steel himself – happened to be the *Nationalblad*'s largest creditor. So it was up to him to tackle the not so simple assignment of straightening out his affairs. The general opinion was that he was successful, but not without personally suffering considerable losses. For this reason – much against his will – he suddenly had a controlling interest in the *Nationalblad*. What on earth was he supposed to do with it, now that he had promised his support to a new paper? The solution was simple: Levini and Donckert and the other boys could take over the *Nationalblad* and transform it into the paper of their dreams! One evening he explained his ideas to Doncker, Olof Levini and Torsten Hedman. At first they reacted with silence.

'Won't that be a little difficult?' Torsten Hedman said.

'Difficult? Pah!' Henry Steel answered. 'Nothing is really impossible. You simply have to do the best you can. I'll do the best I can and that's the only way I can do it. Just think about it: whatever else can I do with the *Nationalblad*? Those who control the shares in a business have a certain amount of responsibility to keep their employees from suddenly landing on the street without a crust to eat. If you were to become part of this arrangement, then at least the office, printing personnel and the more subordinate and colourless part of the editorial office could stay and keep their jobs. As far as the others are concerned, I'll have to provide for them until they find new jobs.'

'Well, I guess there's nothing else to say,' Olof Levini sighed.

'Besides, the idea is brilliant,' Doncker said. 'This way we get a number of subscriptions to start out with and, according to the laws of inertia, a good many of them are going to stay despite our change in politics!'

The whole affair was taken care of in a hurry at an extraordinary shareholder's meeting.

'You will vote for thirty shares,' Doncker told Henrik Rissler.

And Rissler went to the shareholders meeting in the 'Oscar room' at the restaurant Rydberg and voted for thirty shares he had never seen.

So, that was the history of the paper, as Markel told Arvid Stjärnblom one evening.

Arvid stood at the window in Torsten Hedman's room. He was allowed to use it when it was free. He didn't have anything left to do and was just about to leave – he had left the door open. It was dusk already and it was snowing heavily outside.

He stood there and thought about his future. During the Christmas holidays, when school was closed, he had devoted all of his time to working at the paper and he had enjoyed it. He realized that he could learn more there than during a trial year at the school. Life in the editorial office was much more central, much more part of the world than life at school. Now, in just a couple of days, school would start again. He felt more and more like writing to the principal that, as a result of this and that reason, he was forced to interrupt his trial year. He didn't like doing it since the principal had been very friendly and shown him a lot of interest and complimented him on his pedagogic capabilities. 'Born to be a teacher,' he had said – which had actually scared Arvid somewhat... There was also something else: one day he had exchanged a few words with Dr Doncker and had understood that when Doncker had promised him a regular salary he had completely forgotten that Arvid was doing his trial year at North Latin School. 'Oh,' he had said when Arvid reminded him, 'forget your teaching career, Mr Stjärnblom, unless moiling and toiling for a crust of bread for the rest of your life appeals to you very much...' Then there was something more: the economic basis of the *Nationalblad* was sort of teetering. The paper did improve after the 'revolution', there was no doubt about that, but people at the editorial office were talking among themselves about how the new money the banker Steel had invested had been eaten up a long time ago. Doncker's estimates had been much too sanguine. Even though Steel had calculated with that in mind, it had been an unprecedented situation. At least, Markel said so. One day, Markel had said to Torsten Hedman: 'Today is an exciting day, it's payday! Doncker is riding around in a cab drumming up money for us. One thing you can say about him is that he's decent!'

Arvid was at a loss...

And the snow kept falling...

Well, he might as well go. But first there was something he wanted to talk about with Markel.

He went out into the corridor. It was dark. He turned on a light. At the other end of the corridor he saw a young lady with one of the janitor's boys, who was pointing with his hand, there, that way...

He realized right away that it was Lydia.

She came towards him:

'I wanted to leave an advertisement...but I got lost...'

Arvid stood there, bewildered.

'I can show you the way,' he said.

'Thanks.'

'But are you in a hurry? The advertising office is going to be open for another couple of hours. Would you...wouldn't you like to come to my room for a while?'

It took Lydia a moment to answer.

'If that's all right,' she said.

'Yes, it is,' he answered. 'I use Torsten Hedman's room when he isn't here. He left an hour ago and won't return until after the theatre tonight.'

He pulled the door shut slowly behind them. The room was getting dark. Outside the snow kept falling.

They stood silent and bewildered: both of them. And then they fell into each other's arms and kissed. It was a long kiss.

She was wet from the snow.

'Would you like to take off your coat and hat?' he asked.

'Is that all right? Someone might come in...it would look strange...'

Arvid turned the key in the lock.

'Yes,' he said, 'it's all right. Nobody will come in.'

Neither of them said anything for two, three seconds.

'Is this where you sit and write?' she asked.

'Yes,' he said, 'when Mr Hedman isn't here. When he is here I sit in the big editorial office and write in the company of five or six other pennyless hacks.'

She took off her coat and hat and stood there in her plain black mourning suit and blonde hair.

'But if someone...if someone should need you for something and try to open the door...?'

'Don't worry, Lydia,' Arvid answered. 'The people who work here don't respect much, but one thing that is respected unconditionally is a closed door. But what's this advertisement you were talking about?'

'I'm looking for work. Just about anything will do. Help in a household. I don't have any special talents. Housework is the only thing I can do.'

They were both silent. The snow kept falling and it was getting darker. The first lantern was lit outside and it brightened the ceiling of the room.

'Tell me,' Arvid said, 'do you remember that we met unexpectedly in Djurgården one day last autumn. You were with a gentleman…'

'Yes,' she answered. 'That was Dr Roslin.'

'You mean Markus Roslin, the archeologist and art historian…?'

'Yes, he's an old family friend.'

They were silent. The snow continued to fall.

'I'm going to tell you something,' she said. 'That same afternoon I felt such an irresistible longing to see you. I went up to where you live and rang the doorbell. Nobody opened the door.'

She had whispered this with her blonde head pressed against his chest. He stroked her hair with his hand.

'I was at home,' he said, 'but you only rang once. And I had no idea that it was you.'

'I don't like to ring more than once,' she said. 'I too "respect a closed door…"'

'Oh, Lydia…'

He took her head between his hands and looked into her eyes:

'May I ask you a question?' he said.

'Yes?'

'You must promise me that you won't be angry.'

'Yes?'

'Are you still an "innocent" girl?'

'Of course.'

'Are you angry with me for asking?'

She smiled with tears in her eyes:

'No.'

They were both silent again. It was getting darker and darker. The snow kept falling. She sat with her head resting against his chest. He whispered her name, again and again, senselessly: Lydia…Lydia…Lydia…

Again he took her head in his hands and looked deep into her eyes:

'You will be my guardian angel,' he said. 'Do you want to be my guardian angel?'

Gently she took his hands away.

'I want to be everything for you,' she said, 'but it isn't only what I want… Do you know what I thought when I received your letter? I thought, well, now I have nothing to save myself for…'

'What do you mean…?'

'Oh – nothing…'

It was getting very dark. And the snow continued to fall.

'Lydia. You do understand that I can't think of marriage except as a distant prospect, don't you?'

'Yes.'

'But if you wanted to be my little beloved girl in secret?'

Her eyes looked into the dark, large and full of tears.

'No,' she said. 'I don't want to be a burden to you. Anything else, but not that! Not a burden.'

The white snowflakes danced and glittered and sank to the ground.

They were silent.

'Can you tell me what is right and what is wrong?'

Arvid considered.

'I don't know,' he answered. 'This morning, here at the paper, we translated Zola's "J'accuse", and right now it is most likely being distributed in town as an extra edition. In that particular case I know what is right and what is wrong. But I would have a pretty hard time if I one day found myself having to explain to the boys in school what is right and what is wrong – to give a general explanation, I mean…'

She sat there with her head against his chest and sobbed and sobbed. She hadn't listened to a word of what he had said. She was shaking and sobbing. Then she suddenly got up and dried her tears.

She stood there, young and slender, in her black mourning suit and her light hair.

'I have to go,' she said.

He got up too and, after a long kiss, he said:

'I believe that you will be my guardian angel.'

She put on her hat and coat. They were still wet.

'Goodbye,' she said.

'Can I see you some time?'

'I don't know…'

She stood with her hand on the doorknob – Arvid had unlocked it.

'I don't know,' she said again.

Suddenly she wrapped her arms around his neck:

'I want to whisper something in your ear,' she said.

And she whispered with her mouth very close to his ear:

'I want to. But I don't dare.'

And she loosened her arms and rushed out.

One morning in April, Arvid received a letter. He immediately recognized Lydia's handwriting on the envelope and tore it open feverishly. It contained only one small piece of paper. On one side she had made a pencil drawing of a landscape – a flat autumnal landscape with naked willow skeletons that were reflected in a calm lake, a heavy sky, showers and a flock of migrating birds...

And on the back she had written, also in pencil:

'I want to go away, oh so far, far away.'*

Nothing else. Nothing more.

He stood there wondering, the small piece of paper in his hand. What was it she wanted to tell him? He felt that it was something very special. But what?

Was she planning to take a trip?

'I want to go away, oh so far, far away.'

No, he couldn't understand what she meant. But he put the small piece of paper into his notebook.

*

There were some beautiful early spring days in April that year. When you walked a short distance outside of the city, the roads were still edged by high banks of dirty snow – winter remained, ailing and dying. But inside the city the streets were clean and shining in the sun. The waters of the Norrström glittered, rushed and foamed, and in Kungsträdgården the first poor, swarthy little

* '*Ud vil jeg, ut, a saa langt langt*': a quotation from 'Over The High Mountains' by the Norwegian poet Bjørnstjerne Bjørnson.

Italians were selling small red, blue and green balloons – it was almost as if spring had really come.

One afternoon, about three o'clock, Arvid was walking down one of the paths in Kungsträdgården. Suddenly he saw Philip Stille. They stopped and talked and then walked on together.

'Thanks for your wreath,' he said, 'it was really very kind of you.'

'You're welcome...'

'Are you still at North Latin School doing your training year?'

'No, I've stopped. I suppose you know that I have a job at the *Nationalblad*?'

'Yes, but I thought all the same that... Well, that sort of a career is better, I suppose.'

In the distance they saw two tall gentlemen – everyone on the path was bowing and taking off their hats. It was the King, together with the Master of the Hunt.

They were both silent. Philip seemed to be the kind of person who was impressed by the proximity of a king. Arvid had nothing to say. When the King passed by they bared their heads.

'Have you heard from your brother?' Arvid asked

'Yes, he has a good job over there, in a large engineering firm. He'll be all right. Furthermore,' he continued, 'it turned out that the estate was not in as bad a shape as we had thought. We knew Father hadn't been able to put away any savings, but he didn't have any debts either, which we knew as well. He also had a small collection of "old masters", most of them rather obscure or unknown, which he had acquired for almost nothing over the years, and some of them brought in quite a bit of money at the Bukowski auction. There were a few other art objects and trinkets. The whole thing amounted to nearly to eight thousand crowns. Not a great deal, particularly when you divide it by three. However, the two of us brothers are now able to earn our own living. And Lydia will manage.'

They separated at the corner of Arsenalsgatan. Stille was on his way to Östermalm, Arvid wasn't going anywhere for the moment, but had said that he was going to his office.

'Lydia will manage.' He had said that almost enigmatically, and with a somewhat secretive little smile…

The bells of Jakob's Church were ringing. An old money lender was being buried.

On Jakob's Square he passed by three of the 'Masters of the Kingdom' as they were called in the old days: the former Prime Minister and the Minister of Justice on one side and the War Minister, the thin, dried-up veteran of the Franco-Prussian war, on the other. He had seen them a couple of times before from the reporters' gallery in the old, soon to be condemned Parliament building. He had to smile when he thought about the crazy stories, worthy of Boccaccio, that were circulating about the Minister of Justice, a terribly ugly old man.

A few steps behind them trotted Jörgen, with his whiskers dyed black and his goatee white, dressed in a yellowish grey overcoat that came down to his ankles.

Arvid stopped for a moment on Gustav Adolf Square outside the *Nationalblad* telegraph office, where the telegrams were spread out in the window. The latest read: 'THE POPE HAS OFFERED TO INTERVENE BETWEEN SPAIN AND THE UNITED STATES'. He saw them as if in a dream: Leo XIII's ironic profile, finely chiseled by an unusually long life, the way he remembered it from some reproduction of Lenbach's famous portrait, and McKinley, faithful automatic speechmaking machine for American big business, the mouthpiece for all those about to make money from the war. I'm afraid, he thought, that those two gentlemen will find it difficult to understand each other…and in the background he could see some muddleheaded, half-crazy Spanish statesmen and generals for whom 'the honour of Spain', which means their own, was all, and all of the realities in the world nothing at all… No, he decided, Leo XIII will not be able to prevent that war…

He felt a hand on his shoulder:

'Hello, my boy!'

It was Baron Freutiger.

'Hello... Are you in town?'

'Yes, looks that way. Do you want to come with me to the Rydberg? We can have a glass of wine, or absinthe, or whatever you would like. It's too early for dinner.

They went to the Rydberg and sat down on the leather-covered seats looking out on to Gustav Adolf Square where you could see everybody walking by. Arvid had sat there alone on the same leather-covered seat a few times during the winter, with a glass of port or something – and had stared at the many unknown and the few known faces and bodies walking by in snow and rain. This was the first time he had sat there in beautiful and unusually spring-like April weather.

'Absinthe?' Freutiger wanted to know.

'Why not?' Arvid answered.

The absinthe was brought to the table.

Freutiger looked out at the square:

'There goes Dagmar Randel,' he said. 'She's a sweet girl, but already a little too flirtatious. She's having a little flirt right now with Lieutenant Warberg. And there goes Märta Brehm. A very stylish girl! She supposedly has a child with a medical student whose name is Tomas Weber – a real nincompoop, actually...'

Arvid listened absentmindedly. What did those names, which he had never heard before, have to do with him? In Karlstad, at least, he knew all of the town's girls as far as their looks and reputations were concerned, but here he knew almost no one!

'I think you're forgetting that I'm from the country,' he said

'Yes, but for God's sake, you're not always going to be from the country!' Freutiger replied.

'Was that Snoilsky who just went by?' Arvid asked.

He thought he had recognized the famous poet from pictures he had seen.

'Of course. I'll tell you a story, unless you have already heard it. Ibsen had a birthday a few weeks ago – seventy or eighty or whatever it was – and he went on his so-called 'grand cross tour' of his 'sister' countries: first to Copenhagen, where he was decorated with the grand cross of Dannebrog and celebrated and honoured with speeches and a torchlight procession, after which he got drunk, then to Stockholm, where he was celebrated and awarded the grand cross of the North Star and honoured with a gala presentation and speeches, after which he got drunk. One morning Snoilsky paid him a visit at the Grand Hotel. He found him sitting at a table, and on the table lay the grand crosses with their accoutrements. He sat there looking at them with his grave, grim eyes. "Well, my dear Henrik Ibsen," said Snoilsky, "of all Scandinavian writers you are certainly the one who has received the most of that sort of a thing." – "I should hope so!" Ibsen answered. – "Except perhaps Oehlenschläger," Snoilsky continued. Ibsen wrinkled his brow. At that point Snoilsky noticed the grand cross of St Olav lying among the others. "Yes, I suppose that's right," Snoilsky said, "Oehlenschläger couldn't very well receive the St Olav." – "I should hope not!"

'That's a good story,' Arvid answered, 'but I think it's travelled by many stations before it got to you – and you as well are a "station" and certainly not one of the worst. Skoal!'

'Do you mean to say that I'm sitting here lying to you?'

'Of course not. You never lie: that I know. But wouldn't you like me to try and reconstruct the episode in the way it might have happened?'

'Very much.'

'Good. Snoilsky comes in. According to your version, Ibsen is sitting there staring at his decorations. But that's simply unthinkable: he is usually described as an utterly formal and ceremonial old gentleman – even when he is drunk, which he wasn't on this occasion. It is completely unthinkable that he could have treated Snoilsky, whom he had known ages ago in Rome, with the least amount of discourtesy. So, he most likely got up and walked towards him and said "good day" or something. His decorations happen to be on the table perhaps, maybe he was just about to pack them in a suitcase. Snoilsky uses them as a subject for conversation, makes some half-humorous remarks. Ibsen answers with his "I should hope so" most likely also a little humorously and ironically, but with more ponderous emphasis because of his more ponderous nature…'

'I don't believe it!' Freutiger burst out. He was leafing through the afternoon paper.

'What…?' Arvid asked.

'Look for yourself!'

He gave him the paper and pointed at an engagement announcement. And Arvid read:

MARKUS ROSLIN
AND
LYDIA STILLE

'What do you make of that?' Freutiger said. 'That girl doesn't go in for small potatoes! Markus Roslin – at least six hundred thousand.'

Arvid didn't say anything. At that moment he was happy to let Freutiger talk. That way he didn't have to say anything himself. He was afraid his voice would give him away.

'Can you imagine, Arvid: she is the only girl I have ever loved – seriously, you understand! Two weeks after old man Stille died I wrote to her and proposed. Honorably and according to the rules, I think, with the exact size of my fortune: a little bit more than two hundred thousand. She answered immediately and signed herself "Respectfully Yours". You can imagine the contents of the letter. Well, I thought, of course, that she considered me too old – forty-six and she nineteen – and couldn't help admiring her steadfastness when offered the chance of being supported for the rest of her life. But Roslin is over fifty. So it wasn't my age that was the problem. It wasn't that at all!'

'My dear Freutiger,' Arvid said – he heard his voice as though it were someone else's, from far away – 'do you seriously think that the difference in fortunes is what made her decide? Money is necessary for living, but a little more, a little less – I'm sure she didn't think that way...' Freutiger passed his hand over his eyes.

'Well, no, I don't suppose she did. I guess she just felt that Roslin cut a better figure than I. Besides, she can expect to be widowed a few years earlier with him than with me – I certainly hope she manages to finish him off quickly, poor guy, he's not that strong... Her being in love with him is completely impossible. Come, have dinner with me, we'll eat well and drink ourselves under the table!'

'Thanks, but I can't,' Arvid answered. 'I have to get to the paper by five o'clock.'

He wanted to be alone.

At that time of day he had nothing to do at the editorial office, but he went there anyway.

He walked through some of the rooms. They were all empty.

He stopped next to the window in Torsten Hedman's room. It was stuffy. He opened it.

From a backyard nearby an organ was playing. It was playing 'Kväsarvalsen', a popular hit of the day.

His beloved – the one whom he had kissed at twilight behind the lilac hedge – his beloved...

'I want to go away, oh so far, far away.'

What it had meant was: wedding trip to the Riviera, Italy, perhaps Egypt...

He stood there and babbled those words over and over again: 'I want to go away, oh so far, far away.'

His eyes fell on the sofa. They had sat there – and, at the door, when she was about to leave, she had said:

'I want to! But I don't dare!'

Suddenly he remembered what he was thinking that time she had said: 'I can wait'. He hadn't wanted anyone to wait for him.

Now he had what he wanted. There was no one waiting for him. No one at all.

Howling like a wild animal he threw himself on to the sofa.

PART II

'You do not choose your destiny
any more than you choose your wife,
your lover or your children.
You get them, and you have them, and
possibly you lose them.
But you do not choose them!'

Years passed.

Arvid Stjärnblom worked for the paper. After one year he had become the regular music critic. After that evening when by chance he had reviewed Miss Klarholm's debut as Margareta in Faust, he had, in his free time, read just about everything there was to read about music at the Royal Library. Since he was also somewhat musical he was able to succeed the regular critic, who was unwell a little too often. After two or three years he had a salary of two thousand four hundred crowns a year, with, of course, the obligation to work on everything and anything. The paper's finances were still not so consolidated that they could pay so much just for a music critic. It was improving, however, as anyone could see: subscriptions and ads were increasing and at the same time the paper was growing in size like a woman blessed with the fruit of her womb. Unfortunately, operating expenses were growing on an even larger scale – or so Markel stated. No one quite knew who was paying. Steel had long ago washed his hands of the *Nationalblad*. After him there had been another and then still another and nobody really knew who had the valuable controlling majority... Dr Doncker drove around in a carriage or automobile – he almost never had time nowadays to do any writing – and, on payday, there was always money available.

'Do you remember,' Arvid told Markel on some occasion, 'do you remember what Balzac called newspapers? *Ces lupanars de la pensée*. "The whorehouses of the thinking world".'

'Hmm,' Markel had answered. 'Did he really say that, the old devil?'

'Yes, he did.'

'Did he really say thinking? That's absolutely too charming! But, after all, he was an incurable romantic.'

Right after that, he had added:

'My dear Arvid, you write about music, and whatever else you fancy, for that matter. What are you complaining about? I have all the dirt and all the mischief close up and I don't complain! I do what I can and try to prevent as much nonsense and as many pranks as possible, but when I realize that I'm powerless I have to let it go... You are never forced to write anything against your will, and I don't either. However, as assistant chief and often night editor as well, I often find myself compelled, much against my will, to let through "false reports that confuse the public". You don't have to do that. You simply write about music and whatever else and then pick up your salary. So, what are you complaining about?'

'I'm not complaining either,' Arvid answered. 'I just can't help thinking every time I pick up my salary that without these "false reports that confuse the public" there wouldn't be any money to pay my salary.'

'Oh, my innocent lamb,' said Markel. 'You're not just a moralist. You're a super-moralist. "False reports". My God, they've got to exist. Once again we are faced with Pilate's old question: what is truth?'

'The old hag has been arrested in Madrid!' Markel said as he passed Arvid's room with a box of telegrams in his hand.

The old hag was Mrs Humbert. At that time, around the end of 1902, it was 'the big Thérèse' and her cash register that kept the newspapers and the whole world busy. She even overshadowed the Crown Princess of Saxony and Mr Giron.

Arvid was thinking about other things. It was December 20th. His birthday. On his desk in front of him stood two red roses in a glass. He sat there looking at them, embarrassed and a little moved at the same time. Never before had anyone in this city remembered his birthday.

Actually, he thought he knew whom they were from. To be on the safe side, however, he had asked the boy in the hallway:

'Was it a boy from a florist, or...'

'No, it was a lady.'

'Blonde or dark?'

'Blonde.'

It was just as he had thought: Dagmar Randel. A few weeks ago he had been invited to a dinner and dance for young people at the house of Mr Randel, the property magnate. During a break between dances he had sat and talked with the only unmarried daughter of the family, Miss Dagmar. She had complained that she was getting so terribly old:

'On December 20th I am going to be twenty-six years old,' she had said

'Well, that's really terrible,' he had answered. 'But what am I supposed to say, since I'm going to be twenty-eight on exactly the same day?'

'No, really – do we have the same birthday? That's funny...'

And so on... Since then he had met her only outdoors, fleetingly, and they had exchanged a few indifferent words. Now she had come with these roses.

Strange that she had come here to his office instead of sending them to where he lived...

She must have guessed that he wasn't home very much. She had also wanted to meet him. Strange that she wasn't afraid to take flowers to a man in an editorial office where people run in and out constantly...people might have started talking...

How was he supposed to return her courtesy? Send flowers back? He checked the contents of his purse. There wasn't much money.

He decide to write a short note:

Miss Dagmar Randel,

I thank you for your kindness in remembering a coincidence as unimportant as our having the same birthday – for my part I must blushingly ask you to forgive me because I had forgotten all about it. I can't deny that I was a little moved. During the more or less five years that I have spent in this city no one, so far, has ever asked me about my birthday.

Your grateful,
Arvid Stjärnblom.

While he was putting the letter into an envelope, Markel came in:

'Oh yes,' he said, 'there is something I have to tell you – I happened to see the girl when she was here with the flowers – be careful, for God's sake! Old man Randel's affairs are absolutely rotten!'

'You've already told me that once,' said Arvid. 'But I really don't see what these two *roses* have to do with his affairs.'

'You don't? Those roses cost two crowns each, at least. The girl wants to get married!'

Arvid burst out laughing:

'Please, Markel,' he said, 'do you want to make me believe that I, with my two thousand four hundred crowns a year, could be considered an eligible match?'

'Oh no, she hasn't the slightest idea about things like that – she thinks that her father is a rich man and she herself an eligible match: and she wants to get married! Just be careful, my boy! Besides, I don't have time to talk about such nonsense any longer... Doncker is nervous as hell. He's got wind of a new millionaire, a Rickson! The name alone is worth money! We have to get through the end of the year! But look who's here – Henrik Rissler. What do you want?'

Rissler was standing in the doorway.

'Sell a short story,' he answered. 'Price: fifty crowns, but I'm in a hurry – does Doncker have to read it before I can get the money?'

'Hell, Doncker hasn't the time either to read or write nowadays. If this continues for a few more years he'll be illiterate!'

In a great hurry, Markel wrote out an order for fifty crowns. That was Rissler's rate nowadays. A year ago he had enjoyed a nice little success with a nice little book.

Henrik Rissler left, and Markel as well, but in the doorway he turned around and said:

'Be careful! In the old days it was the man who went looking for a woman. That's old fashioned; now it's the woman who goes looking for a man. And she'll stop at nothing!'

Arvid sat thinking. He thought about that evening at the Randels and how he had been invited. One day in November he had been sitting by himself on one of the leather seats at the Rydberg café, at about three o'clock in the afternoon, watching the shadow play of passers-by outside. Among them he saw Randel, the architect, the property magnate's younger son – the older one had become a pastor. A few moments later, Hugo

Randel came into the café, looked around, saw Arvid was alone and came over to sit with him. They had met a few times in merry company and called each other by their first names.

'I've got something to show you!' Randel had said

He had pulled some drawings out of his pocket. It was a proposal for the redesigning and reconstructing of one of the most central, but ugliest – in terms of buildings and thoroughfares – parts of Stockholm.

Arvid studied the drawings, asked some questions, received answers and tried to understand the details. The whole thing seemed like a good idea to him – whether it was workable or not was difficult to say.

'How do you like it?' Hugo Randel wanted to know.

'Fine – but what does it all mean? Since I don't really understand a lot about this sort of thing.'

'Couldn't you put it into your paper? Of course, I don't want anything for it – just the publicity.'

'Well, I can try. You know, I don't have any influence.'

They were silent for a minute, watching the shadow play outside.

Many people went by. After a while they saw Elin Blücher.

Elin Blücher was a tall, slender, dark-haired girl with a pale and interesting face. He knew hardly anything about her except that her name was Elin Blücher. He had seen her pass by often, and for about six months he had had a secret crush on her.

'That was Elin Blücher,' Hugo Randel said.

'Do you know her?' Arvid asked.

'Oh yes. She's a good friend of my sister Dagmar's and spends lots of time at our house.'

'Awfully handsome girl.'

'Do you think so? Well, to each his own. Do you know her?'

'Not at all. I've only seen her around.'

'If you would like to meet her I can arrange it. We're going to have a dinner and dance for young people at my father's house in about a week or so. If you want to come I'll see that you get an invitation. Then you'll meet Elin Blücher.'

'Well, thanks, why not...? Let me take another look at your proposal.'

He studied the drawings seriously and for a long time.

'I'll do the little I can to get it into the paper,' he said. 'Anything that has to do with changes to the city's appearance is always of interest. You do have some text to go with all these plans and profiles, don't you?'

'Yes, but not with me. I can leave it with you tomorrow. Maybe you can add a little bit of journalistic spice.'

They shook hands and parted. A few days later Hugo Randel's project, together with plans and profiles and text, could be read in the *Nationalblad* and it stirred interest and discussion. A week later Arvid was one of the guests at a dinner and dance for young people at Mr Randel's, the property magnate – who was known as Director Randel

He had indeed met Elin Blücher there, and danced with her and talked with her – about the weather and Mme Hubert's cash register or whatever else. However, the moment he had talked with her the magic was over. She was still a very sweet girl, but entirely different from what he had expected. She was more...more common. She munched sweets and seemed to have nothing else to think about.

However, during the course of the evening he had seen Miss Dagmar Randel's eyes catch his with an expression that seemed to say: 'You look like a nice boy. Would you like to play with me?'

*

Arvid was on his way to the Café du Nord for dinner. Jakob's Church clock said four thirty.

Winter didn't seem to want to start properly – raw, cold, grey days and sometimes a little snow mixed with rain. Arvid was longing for snow. He thought about his distant home where his old father had now sat alone at the Christmas dinner table five winters in a row. He had two brothers, both several years older than him. Herman, the oldest, had come to nothing and, even worse, had been given passage to America and had been gone for many years. The other one, Erik, was a doctor at a hospital on the west coast, and Arvid had not as yet, during the past five years, been able to get away from the paper at Christmas. It, together with the turn of the year, was the busiest time for newspapers, just as it was for the post office and the railroad.

Then he remembered that he still had the letter to Dagmar Randel in his pocket. He walked to the mailbox on the corner of Arsenalsgatan and mailed it. Then he turned around and just at that moment Miss Randel walked by.

He greeted her. She stopped.

'That letter was addressed to you,' he said. 'It was only a thank you note for the flowers. I feel undeserving and very contrite – after all I haven't sent any flowers to you…'

'No, why should you have?' she answered. 'It says neither in the Bible nor the catechism that you're supposed to send flowers on birthdays. You just do it if you feel like it, and I felt like it. Where are you going?'

'I was planning to go to the Café du Nord, for dinner.'

'Are you very hungry?'

'Not really.'

There was a little pause.

'At home we don't dine until six,' she said, 'and it's so annoying to come home too early. Couldn't you take a walk with me? Towards Skeppsholmen?'

They walked by the Grand Hotel, where a reddish light streamed out of the bar, towards the National Museum and the bridge to Skeppsholmen.

On Skeppsholmen they stopped under a black skeleton of a big tree.

He kissed her.

While they were kissing he thought: this is simply an act of courtesy necessary to the situation.

They recovered themselves and stood silently, staring across Strömmen's running, black waters with its sparkling mirrors and spirals of light from the rows of lanterns on the quays.

Suddenly he remembered Markel's words: she wants to get married.

He caressed her hand:

'My dear,' he said, 'do you understand that I can't even think about getting married?'

She looked down and it took a little while for her to answer.

'That's something I hadn't thought about at all,' she said.

They walked a little back and forth on the quay. She said:

'I will make a confession. I really did have a small ulterior motive with the flowers.'

He looked up, questioning. She continued:

'I would so much like to have a job and an independent income. It is so unpleasant to have to ask Father for everything. Couldn't you try to get me a job on the paper? Writing about fashion and society and such?'

Arvid thought about it. For women's fashions they had someone and for society reporting they had a born countess with a historic name.

'That might be a little difficult, but I can always try.'

They walked back across the bridge, arm in arm.

'Tell me,' he said, 'why is it so annoying to come home too early for dinner?'

'It's because everything's annoying at home,' she answered.

He didn't ask any more.

When they said goodbye, she said:

'When will we see each other again?'

Arvid thought about it. Perhaps he could take time off

tonight… Yes, there wasn't anything at the Opera, there was no concert and he didn't really have anything special to do.

So he answered:

'I'm just going to sit at home and be bored all evening. Would you like to come and see me?'

'What time?'

'Seven – can you come at seven?'

'I'll try…'

Arvid went to the Café du Nord and ate dinner. He had meatballs and beans.

In spite of his twenty-eight years, Arvid's sexual experience was very limited.

Except for Mrs Kravatt in Karlstad – whom he still missed from time to time – his experience consisted of a few fleeting encounters with girls who walked the streets at night. He wouldn't be able to recognize them the next day except maybe by their hat or their boa or something, but never by their face. Then there was the sweet little shopgirl four years ago – the time when Lydia Stille got married – whom he managed to get pregnant. That is to say, it wasn't entirely sure. She actually had had a fiancé, but he had disappeared.

This had, of course, been a very serious situation. He had written to his father, his brother Erik and to Freutiger. His father had sent him two hundred crowns out of his meagre income – without a sermon about morality – his brother Erik sent him the same amount, but with a sermon, and from Freutiger he received five hundred. The matter was taken care of for the time being. The child – a boy – he had placed with a decent working class family in Sundbyberg, and the mother, thanks to a recommendation from Freutiger, found herself a better job than the one she had been in before, and was doing well. Arvid paid thirty-five crowns a month for the child.

After that incident he had resolved that never ever, without exception, would he again seduce a 'poor' girl. The possibility of a 'rich' girl hadn't even entered his mind. He would capitulate to necessity, putting up with the life of a bachelor – a penniless bachelor, with the unavoidable dirt and disgust – until the day when he was able to have a home and a family, and had found the one he wanted to have a home and family with.

And now that his resolution had been put to the test for the first time, he had immediately yielded to temptation – made an 'exception'. It was, after all, something entirely different with Dagmar Randel. He could in this case hardly adorn himself with the glory of the seducer. Since she had offered him her young, luxurious, blonde beauty he would have been an idiot had he not accepted...

She had, of course, asked the obligatory question first: 'Do you love me?'

And, of course, he had answered: 'I love you.' For otherwise this couldn't be happening.

Love and love...

He had already lost his 'first heart', as it was called. He had this idea that at least seven years had to pass before he could grow a new one. Nevertheless, one's natural impulses do not remain dormant – far from it. What he was offered now was really a paradise compared to what he was used to. Therefore he had said: 'I love you.' But meant: I can't love you; but I can make love to you; make the gestures and do the pantomime.

Almost every day she sneaked her way up to his room, preferably around seven or eight o'clock in the evening. He was now living in a furnished room on Grevturegatan. Just before ten he would take her back to the entrance of her house. Then he would go to the Rydberg or the Café du Nord to have a couple of drinks, or else he would go to his office. One day he said to Markel:

'By the way, you were mistaken about Miss Randel's purpose with those flowers. She didn't want to get married. She wanted a job with the newspaper.'

'Well, that was comparatively innocent,' Markel replied.

*

During the course of a year Arvid usually exchanged only a few letters with his father, and they were short; but every New Year's Eve he wrote longer and more detailed reports. He did so now, on New Year's Eve 1902. He wrote:

Dear Father,

With all my heart, I wish you a good new year. My wages will continue to be the same during the new year, but Dr Doncker has promised me a little vacation next summer and I hope that then, for the first time in six years, I will be able to see again my beloved childhood home.

During the past autumn I have begun to be admitted into a small corner of Stockholm society. I've been invited to dinner a few times at the house of Consul-General Rubin – it was, of course, Markel who introduced me. You meet many different sorts of people there – the Consul-General entertains in grand style, and that's always interesting. I've also been invited to Director Randel's – perhaps you have seen his name in the paper from time to time, in connection with different projects. Even Professor Levini was kind enough to invite me one evening, but unfortunately I was busy with something new at the Opera. That was almost the greatest mortification in my life, this past autumn. And now, between Christmas and New Year, I've been out on the island at Freutiger's for a couple of days.

As far as my financial affairs are concerned, as you know, I have repaid Erik the two hundred. (Markel lent me one hundred of that, despite the fact that he is not very well off.) But I still owe Freutiger those five hundred.

For us hacks, Christmas Eve is one of the few holidays of the year. In the morning I went out to Sundbyberg to visit my little boy. He resembles our family – there is something about his eyes and forehead, something I can't describe but which makes me certain of the fact that he is my boy.

About the Union: dear father, you know, of course, that my view is very different from yours. I think that you are very unfair towards old Jean-Baptiste when you scold him for the fact that he didn't make Norway into a Swedish province in 1814. First of all, I doubt that he had the power to do so. Secondly, I doubt that it would have done us any good. Thirdly, he wasn't alone with his opinion; he shared it with Adlersparre and Järta and others of the 'men of 1809'. But he was alone in one thing in the Sweden of that time: he had the ability to do what was done! If his successors – by which I don't only or even especially mean his successors on the throne, but the whole class of Swedish leaders to this day – have botched his accomplishments, he can certainly not be blamed for that!

As the situation has developed now, the Union has become a weakness and a danger for Sweden. Norway wants to get out of the Union: everything points to that – the consular conflict is just the form or excuse chosen or offered for the time being. The way things are developing, Norway is going to make use of the first favourable opportunity – for example, a possible war with Russia – to stab us in the back. As things are now, a Union is simply meaningless or worse. Yes, to hold on to the status quo, as the Boström government seems to want to do, will work for a while, most likely, as long as the present king is alive; but it won't work for any length of time. As things are now, the Union should be dissolved, and Sweden should take the initiative. You see this kind of thinking here and there in the conservative press, but only in the form of small outbursts of temper and anger – instead, the government should make a formal statement about it. The addition of defensive forces that (on paper) the Union means for Sweden is ridiculously small, while on the other hand the ambiguity and uncertainty in our relationship with Norway could spell disaster at a critical time.

By 'ambiguity' I mean the following: it says in the first paragraph of the constitution and likewise in the first paragraph of the Norwegian constitution that Norway 'shall be a free and independent state'. However, the factual constitutional position according to the continuation of the same constitution is that they are autonomous but not sovereign.

Dear Father: as a Swede you would certainly not be completely satisfied with such a situation for Sweden. Can you, then, blame the Norwegians for not being entirely delighted with theirs?

Your son,
Arvid.

The year 1903 left no lasting impression on the history of the world. It was the year Sweden relinquished the duchy of Mecklenburg, its pawned Right of Sovereignty over the city of Wismar. It was the year Leo XII died, and Cardinal Sarto became Pope. It was the year Alexander and Draga of Serbia were murdered and Black Peter became King!

And it was the year, when…

★

Arvid worked at his newspaper. And went through the gestures and the pantomime of love. Since, however, he had been born with the desire to try to make the best of everything, including the crumbs of happiness life offered him, he sometimes managed to convince himself that he loved Dagmar. Convincing her was easy.

There was never any talk of marriage – almost never. Dagmar had touched on the issue only once during the whole winter and spring.

It was one evening in May – he remembered, because on the same day he had been to Snoilsky's funeral and reported on it for the newspaper.

It was dusk, they were on their way to her door on Engelbrektsgatan and had stopped in the deep shade under Humlegården's old trees.

She said:

'I understand so very well that you don't want to marry. Almost all marriages nowadays are unhappy. But tell me: is it really only because you can't afford it?'

It took him a while to answer.

'I have never said that I don't want to,' he answered. 'I said that I can't.'

'Yes, but,' she looked down, her eyes almost closed, 'Father has told me that if I marry he will contribute two thousand a year to my household, the same as he does for Eva and Margit.'

Eva and Margit were her two married sisters.

'Dagmar,' he answered, 'I don't want to be in a position of being economically dependent on your father. After all, up to now I have been able to take care of myself, more or less.'

Then he added, with a feeling that every word could be important:

'Since you wanted to know…I want to be completely honest with you. It isn't only the fact that I can't afford it. There is also something else. I have such a strong and absolute need to be alone. That, of course, doesn't mean that I need to be alone all day long. I want to have the right to begin and especially end my day by myself. To think by myself and to sleep by myself. I don't think that I am suited for marriage and family life.'

They stood there silently for a few moments. From a nearby bench they could hear two voices whispering. A woman's voice: 'But you promised…' And a man's voice: 'Well yes, but one promises so much…'

Arvid and Dagmar smiled at each other.

'We, at least, haven't promised each other anything,' he said. 'And don't you agree that it is best that way?'

'Yes,' she answered. 'And I really understand you so well.'

He took her to her door. Then he went to his office. In Torsten Hedman's room, which he still used whenever it was free, he found Professor Levini sitting at the desk.

'Excuse me,' the Professor said, 'am I taking up your space? I'll be finished in a minute.'

'That's all right, Professor... May I just use the telephone for a moment.'

He called down to the basement and asked for a copy of his funeral report.

'That's right,' said Professor Levini, 'you were at the funeral – what a scandal, don't you think? Awful! I mean, the pastor! It was almost worse – in a way – than eight years ago when he talked rubbish over Viktor Rydberg's corpse in Klara's Church and assigned him to a space in the "forecourt" – as if he had the keys to the holy of holies himself! And as a reward – it used to be called "the corpse's chair" in the old days – he got Viktor Rydberg's chair at the Academy!

A boy from the printing shop came up with the copy.

'May I see?' said Professor Levini.

'Please.'

Levini eyed the paper hastily. When he reached the report on the pastor's speech he smiled into his black beard. The pastor's speech was reported briefly and concisely and without comment. 'As a testimony to Carl Snoilsky's warm piety the preacher pointed out that the dying poet had allowed without protest the singing of psalms in the corridors and staircases of the hospital... The preacher ended by expressing a warm hope that the deceased poet who during his life had been so close to his earthly King may come to be just as close to the King of heaven.'

'It's appalling,' said Professor Levini. 'Yes, you can laugh about it, Mr Stjärnblom – but you have to realize one thing: that fantastic fossil sits in the Swedish Academy and is one of those who make decisions about who gets the Nobel Prize!'

Suddenly Markel was standing in the doorway:

'Well,' he said, 'that's the least of our troubles. Who cares about who wins the Nobel Prize? Nobel's testament was idiotic, and trying to execute it in a reasonable way presents an insoluble problem. But, Arvid, I do have a few words to say to you privately. Come in here!'

He pulled Arvid into a half-dark room, the 'foreign minister's office, and closed the door to the other room.

'Sit down,' he said. 'Miss Dagmar Randel has been here three or four times recently and asked for you. There must, therefore, be something going on between you and her. I suggest that there are three possibilities. The first one is that you are madly in love with her. If that is so, then I will simply shut up and wait and see. I find this possibility quite believable: she's a sweet girl, and you haven't been especially spoiled, after all…'

'My dear Markel – what the hell do you have to do with Miss Randel?'

'Don't interrupt me. The next possibility is that you think she would be a good match. But I really don't think that you are that much of an idiot. More likely the first possibility is connected and mixed up with the second: that you are a little bit in love and believe you'd get a good match out of it…'

'Really, Markel, this is going too far – what is it to you?'

Markel was silent for a couple of seconds.

'Nothing,' he answered a little drily. 'Actually, it has nothing at all to do with me. But if you happen to walk down a street and meet a runaway horse and impulsively throw yourself in its path to stop it, you would perhaps be somewhat taken aback if the gentleman in the carriage screams at you: "What the hell is it to you…?"'

Arvid had to laugh:

'That simile is rather lame,' he said. 'I can't very well be both the horse and the gentleman in the carriage, can I?'

'It's not lame at all,' Markel answered. 'You are both the horse and the gentleman in the carriage! Shall we proceed as Kant would? Stjärnblom *als Erscheinung*: that's the horse, or rather, the horse running away with the carriage, the whole understood as one thing. Stjärnblom *als Ding an sich*: that's the gentleman in the carriage. The horse is Stjärnblom as a member of the sensual world, the gentleman in the carriage is Stjärnblom as a rational being – which means that he doesn't express himself as irrationally as the gentleman in the carriage in question!'

Arvid thought for a while.

'Let's not quarrel, Markel,' he said. 'Perhaps I'm being unjust towards you by dealing with this matter in such a formal manner. Besides, I can reassure you by honestly saying that there is nothing in my mind about making a good "match".'

'Good,' Markel answered. 'In that case we have reached the third possibility. Which is that she is in love with you, while you are not in love with her – except in the way any normal man is in love with a well-shaped woman – and that you are using her and her love to satisfy your lust. That's human. But it's also mean! You can't do that sort of a thing! Let's bring up Kant again: never make use of a human being – never only make use of a human being! That is simply mean!'

Arvid felt weak.

'You are wrong,' he said. 'It is more complicated than you think. I can't find a solution. But since we've started to talk about it, I'd quite like to know what sort of a reason you have for supposing that there is an intimate relationship between Miss Randel and myself?'

'For your part, no reason at all. You never speak about her and if someone mentions her you're silent or else you say, sort of absentmindedly, "Miss Randel". You're discreet and that's quite all right. But what good is it if she is childish and rash enough to send you flowers and to ask for you here...? The messenger boys in the hall are talking about you and her, so what good is your great discretion? You don't want to marry – and you're right, you can't afford it. The point is not what you want, however; the point is what is going to happen! You don't choose! You do not choose your destiny any more than you choose your parents or yourself: your bodily strength, your character, the colour of your eyes, or the convolutions of your brain. Everyone knows that. Just as you don't choose your wife, your lover, or your children. You get them, and you have them, and possibly you lose them. But you do not choose them!'

Arvid was very thoughtful on his way home.

'You don't choose.'

He thought about Markel, who had told him that. 'You don't choose.'

Markel was a bachelor, involved in an old unhappy love relationship with a woman who was no longer young, but nevertheless young enough to deceive him with almost anyone.

*

Summer went by.

Dagmar Randel spent it with her parents – that is, her father and her stepmother – her own mother was dead – at the family country house in the archipelago. Arvid was in town during most of the summer. Two or three times during the course of the summer he was invited out to Randelsborg, which was the name of their little house on Värmdön, but he was busy in town, working. Or rather, he didn't dare; he wanted to visit her family as little as possible. They were amiable and nice enough, but he couldn't trust Dagmar's self-control. He was afraid, for example, that she would thoughtlessly address him out of the blue with *du* or simply that her behaviour towards him would give away that which must and should remain secret.

Besides, she came to town from time to time, so they were able to meet.

In August he went to Värmland and spent a couple of weeks in his childhood home. Everything there was unchanged. As before, the hopbines climbed around the doorway. And as before, the wind whistled among the tall old birches. Nowhere else did birches grow as tall and beautiful as there.

The old man was the same as always, except that his hair was a little whiter than six years ago, and perhaps he was even a little more silent. The conversations between father and son consisted mostly of short interviews – brief questions from the old one and answers that were a little longer.

'Is the boy developing well?'

'Yes, he is smart and sweet. The bookbinder and his wife are delighted with him.

'And his mother?'

'She works in her shop, and I suppose she doesn't have much time to go and see him. I have more things to do in Sundbyberg. The bookbinder binds my books.'

'What does he call you? The boy, I mean.'

'Recently he's learned to call me Papa. He used to call the bookbinder Papa and me uncle.'

'Hmm. How old is he now – four? He's soon going to be of an age when he should belong to a family of his father's class. I certainly would like to have him here; there's fresh air and it's a healthy place for a boy to grow up in. But I'm old and will most likely die soon. I'm afraid old Sara doesn't have much understanding when it comes to children. Of course, she's had one herself, but that was more than fifty years ago...'

Old Sara, the housekeeper, came out with the punch tray.

'Skoal, Arvid.'

'Skoal, Father.'

After a pause;

'How did this actually happen?'

'I was in love,' Arvid answered. 'But not actually with her. I was in love with a girl I couldn't have because I couldn't support her. She married a rich man, and that was right of her. There was a sweet young girl who lived in the same house as me. She was a shop assistant at a haberdasher's on Kungsbacken. I used to buy things from her from time to time. A couple of times when I arrived at closing time we walked home together. We used to kiss on the staircase. That evening, when the one I was in love with was married, I wanted to have a wedding too. So I did.'

'Hmm. Strange morals, nowadays. But then, morals have always been a little strange, for that matter.'

'To her credit, I have to say,' said Arvid, 'that she herself felt right away that it was a chance and casual occurrence. She did have a "fiancé" whom she loved perhaps as much as I loved her, or perhaps not even that... Both women and men are sometimes seized by longings which can't be defined as moral or rational.'

'Yes, yes,' said the old man, 'I do remember hearing about such things.'

There was a short pause.

'So she didn't make any demands of marriage?'

'Not for a minute. She understood it as an accident. Since I – not with my own means, as you well know, Father! – helped her to get over the "accident" the matter was taken care of. Now she sails in her own waters and never tries to have any contact with me. Her "fiancé", whom I have never seen and who moved away as soon as there was a smell of something burning, was probably a very ordinary man. I was, for her perhaps, the guy in the fairy tale, an adventure – who knows? Who knows how life appears in a poor shop assistant's thoughts and dreams? She has never looked for, or tried to contact, me in any way since.'

'Do you ever see her?'

'Very seldom. We met once in Sundbyberg. She's asked me not to shop where she works. She wanted to forget, she said. I usually send her a little present at Christmas.'

'Still, I would really very much like to see your boy,' the old man said. 'And I've thought about something. We have a new pastor, as you know. Ljungberg is his name. He's been married for six years and has no children. He could perhaps take your boy for the same amount a month as the bookbinder, or, if he wants more, I could pay for it. Last year I paid off the last of my old debts, so now I can manage and still have some left over. But you're a freethinker, aren't you? Maybe you don't want your boy to grow up in a pastor's house.'

'That's not so important, so long as he's a good man. I do think that it's best for a child to be raised more or less in the same way as other children of the same country and time. I don't think that it is generally possible to raise a child to have this or that philosophy of life. The effect is often the opposite. It is better to let him, when the time comes, try his hand at finding his own way… But what's he like, this pastor?'

'Nice fellow, not in the least bookish. He's just like everybody else. His wife is quite delicate and melancholy, but otherwise a good human being.'

'I see. Yes, it certainly is something to think about. There's something else, too. In the case of illegitimate children it is always the mother who has the rights. All the father has to do is pay. So it depends upon what she says.'

'All right then, write and ask her!'

Arvid wrote to Alma Lindgren, explained the situation and asked for her opinion.

In the meantime, the old man talked with Pastor Ljungberg and his wife. They wanted very much to take the boy, but as their own child and without being paid.

'He will never agree to that,' Forester Stjärnblom said. 'He'd rather leave the boy with the bookbinder!'

Arvid went to see the pastor to discuss the matter with him personally. The pastor was a man of about forty, sturdily built, with a good-natured and intelligent face. His wife was a friendly but somewhat pale and thin woman in her thirties.

Arvid said:

'Reverend Ljungberg, I was born here and grew up in this parish and so know that it is very large in size but not in the number of its inhabitants. This consequently affects the size of your income. Because of this, I am, of course, convinced that your kindness over the question of my little boy is dictated by your love of humanity. Generally it is the father who is supposed to provide for his children as much as possible. I have done so up to now and would like to continue doing it.'

'Anna,' the reverend called to his wife, 'could you bring us a little cognac and water?'

They were sitting on a hopbine-covered veranda.

'Yes,' said the reverend. 'That is a point of view I understand and think highly of.'

They agreed on forty crowns a month.

Arvid asked what the reverend's impression of the congregation's morals was.

'Excellent. There's been no murder since 1823, the most recent case of manslaughter occurred in 1896, but could have been called an accident. Theft occurs about once every four years, shoplifting a little more often. Fornication is the one sin that blooms in this parish as much as in all the others; but it simplifies matters: weddings and christenings are combined. Besides, I'm really not so ancient that we can't dispense with titles, am I? I graduated in '81. Skoal, brother!'

'Thanks. Skoal!'

Alma Lindgren's answer came a few days later.

'... I suppose I can't do anything worthwhile for my little Ragnar. It would be wrong of me to go against Arvid and his father over who can make the best possible arrangements for him...'

*

By September he was back in Stockholm.

The first evening Dagmar came to see him after his arrival she could hardly make it into the room before she burst into uncontrollable sobs.

'My dear child... What's the matter, what has happened...?'

She continued sobbing.

Finally she became calm enough to be able to talk:

'My stepmother heard some gossip about us. She immediately went to my father. It wasn't meanness, because she isn't mean, but she lives on gossip. Father became very angry and cross-examined me. First, of course, I thought I'd deny it all, but I was so ashamed and confused I realized I couldn't do it. So I said...'

'Yes? So you said?'

'That we were secretly engaged.'

He was silent. She was silent.

'Well,' she finally said, 'what else should I have said?'

'No – no, of course...it wasn't really possible for you to say anything else. What did your father say?'

'First he called me a bitch and all kinds of other awful names. Then he calmed down and said that he stands by the two thousand a year in case we marry. He didn't say anything bad about you.'

He stood at the window, his hands behind his back, and looked out at the September dusk. 'Secretly engaged'. A single star glimmered dimly in the pale autumn evening sky. So he was secretly engaged now. That was unexpected news...

She slid her arm around his neck and whispered in his ear:

'Is it completely impossible for you to get married?'

'It seems pretty impossible to me, at least,' he answered.

Her arm fell from his neck. Then they were both silent. He stared out into the greying, darkening blue.

Suddenly he heard her sobbing again. She had thrown herself headlong on to the bed.

He went to her and took her head in his hands:

'Don't cry,' he said. 'Please don't cry, my little one! We'll just have to try to do the impossible!'

... And their mouths met in a long kiss.

A few days later, Arvid, dressed in a frock coat, rang the bell at the Randel family's door.

Dagmar received him at the door. She had prepared her father and stepmother for his visit.

In the drawing room he was met by Mrs Hilma Randel, Director Jakob Randel's second wife.

A few years ago her name had been something different and she had been married to someone else. However, when Director Randel became a widower, she divorced her husband in a great hurry and became Mrs Randel. She was about forty years old – dark, rather magnificent and ample, both in the front and the back, and, as far as many gentlemen were concerned, quite seductive. She could be seen at all the premieres, with or without her husband, and at nearly all the public events. A few times her attire had been mentioned in the press. Those were the proudest moments of her life.

She didn't have any children.

Mrs Randel received Mr Stjärnblom with a half motherly, half rather ambiguous smile.

'Yes,' she said, 'little Dagmar has prepared us for your visit. And, after all, it is true, as Anna Norrie sings in *La Belle Hélène*, love is something we must have, even if ever so little... But my husband is waiting for you in his room. Come with me!'

She walked ahead of him and showed the way:

'Jakob!' she called, 'Jaa-kob!'

Director Randel stood in the doorway to his room:

'So, it's Mr Stjärnblom. Welcome. Yes, Dagmar has told me all about it. Would Mr Stjärnblom like a glass of punch?'

'Yes please.'

Director Randel was over sixty. He had a venerable iron-grey patriarch's beard with a white streak on the left-hand side. His hair was white.

'Well,' he said. 'So, Mr Stjärnblom is a journalist. Apparently that isn't as bad nowadays as it used to be. But at any rate...well...two thousand four hundred a year, and I'll give you two thousand, that makes four thousand four hundred, which is a bit meagre. However, young people shouldn't be too pretentious. Let's dispense with titles to begin with. You can call me uncle. Skoal!'

'Skoal, Uncle!'

'Skoal! The newspaper, the one you write for, is it doing well?'

'Quite well.'

'I met Doncker at a dinner a few days ago. He wanted me to buy shares in the paper.'

'This puts me into a so-called conflict of interest,' Arvid said. 'As co-worker on the paper, I should advise Uncle to buy the shares. But as Uncle's possible son-in-law, I have to advise against it!'

'Well, I don't have anything to buy them with anyway! I don't have a penny! Times are bad. Let me show you a painting that I bought on a trip to Paris a few months ago.'

He turned on the electric light to reveal a hackneyed and vulgar painting of a naked woman on a divan.

'What do you think? Isn't it delicious? It's by a famous artist.'

'I see...'

'Would you like to see my decorations?' Director Randel wanted to know. He went to a secretaire, pulled down the lid and opened a little drawer.

He had two 'real' decorations: the Vasa and the St Olav. He displayed them in their cases from Carlberg, the jeweller. In addition, he was a member of a number of private societies – the Order of Carpenters, the Coldinu Order, the Order of Neptune... And he pulled out long ribbons and stars, ribbons in all the colours of the rainbow...

And finally:

'This is the secret drawer, you understand! It contains my Masonic insignia. But those I won't show you! No one is allowed to see them!'

'I'm not that interested,' answered Arvid.

'That's good. But you must become a member of the

Freemasons; one should do that when young. You can get ahead that way. But do you have any idea about what those Norwegians are making a fuss about? After all, they have just as much freedom as we have, more even. They're just too well off, that's what's wrong. Last winter I said to the King at a Masonic function: Your Majesty should move half a million Norwegians to Sweden and half a million Swedes, preferably socialists, to Norway and get them to marry each other willy-nilly, so that they'll become one people!'

'What did the King say to that?'

'Oh, he just laughed. Hmm. But that wasn't what we were supposed to be talking about. Do you have any debts?'

'They're so insignificant that I'm ashamed to speak of them...'

'No, just speak out!'

'Dear Uncle,' Arvid replied, 'I have never for a moment thought that you should be bothered with this... I owe one of my friends five hundred crowns, that's all. Please, Uncle, let this be a matter between my friend and myself...'

'That's out of the question! I will take care of it. My son-in-law should not have any debts! Who did you borrow from?'

'Herman Freutiger...'

'So you know him? He's a fine old boy, I know him from the Brotherhood...'

Mrs Randel put her head round the door:

'Well,' she asked sweetly, 'are you gentlemen reaching any conclusions? Supper is served!'

Director Randel stood up with dignity.

'Ask Dagmar to come in,' he said.

Dagmar came in, blushing.

'All right, my little girl,' said Director Randel, 'you can have the man you want. I hope that you two will make each other happy. Most of all I want to tell both of you something very important, it's a little stanza from the old psalm:

Thou shalt not commit adultery
For that begets great affliction

'Those are words of truth, I know from experience. Hmm! Now let's have a drink and a sandwich!'

The engagement was announced at a big dinner and dance at Randel's on Dagmar's name day. The most distinguished guest – the one who led the hostess to the table – was Cabinet Minister Lundström, a distant relative of Dagmar's mother, Director Randel's first wife. Director Randel had also asked Arvid to suggest a couple of people from the paper. As a result, Doncker and Markel were among the guests. Otherwise, there were Jakob Randel's children and sons and daughters-in-law as well as the closest relatives. Pastor Harald Randel, the oldest son, with his wife, née Platin, and his wealthy in-laws: the stockbroker Platin and his wife. And Hugo Randel, the architect, with his wife and wealthy father-in-law. And Dagmar's sisters, Eva von Pestel with her husband, a lieutenant in the Crown Prince's hussars, and Margit Lindman and her husband, the promising young stockbroker. And many others... Freutiger as well.

After dinner, Markel tried to start a conversation about the Norwegian question with Cabinet Minister Lundström.

'Mm-hmm,' answered Cabinet Minister Lundström.

Then there was dancing...

Arvid and Markel walked together for a while on their way home.

Markel said:

'Perhaps I was informed wrongly about your father-in-law's financial situation. I thought he was going to be on the ropes any time now. Possibly he can keep himself afloat for another couple of years what with his relations and other connections. But certainly not for very long...'

They separated at a street corner:

'I suppose you were right, by the way,' said Arvid. 'You don't choose!'

'No, you don't. Goodnight!'
'Goodnight!'

Arvid went home.

As usual, he wound his watch and hung it from its little nail on the wall over his bed. He placed his keys, purse and wallet and notebook on his bedside table. A little piece of paper fell from the notebook to the floor.

He picked it up. A small pencil drawing. An autumnal landscape with naked willows and a still, grey lake and flights of migratory birds under a cloudy sky. And on the back of it: 'I want to go away, oh so far, far away.'

He thought about it. Year in, year out, the little pencil drawing and those few words had been with him, passing from one notebook to the next – and, certainly, during these years he must have used up at least fifty notebooks.

'I want to go away, oh so far, far away.'

He put it into a bureau drawer – where he kept small relics.

*

The wedding was on the February 10th, 1904. That was the day the paper boys were rushing around the streets in a heavy snowstorm shouting about their extra edition:

RUSSIA AND JAPAN AT WAR!

PART III

'After all, you should be
allowed, just once in your poor
life, to seek your own
Taunitzer Lake...'

Arvid and Dagmar Stjärnblom lived a very happy life together. In December 1904 a little daughter was born. She was christened Anna Maria. At the christening there was a little mishap, but luckily it was easily remedied:

A crystal bowl, one of the wedding gifts, had been placed on a little table, and behind it stood the pastor – it was Harald Randel. The guests were standing in a half circle. The pastor began:

'In name of God, the Father, the Son and the Holy Ghost, amen!

Here he paused and bent over the bowl:

'But,' he added, 'should we not also have a little water in the bowl…? It's true, the water,' he continued with an almost celestial smile, 'doesn't have any effect, but it's still part of the ceremony…'

Arvid took the bowl and rushed to fill it.

The next autumn another little girl was born. She was named Astrid; and that time there was water in the bowl.

That was the year in which the Union broke up, the King cried, and E. G. Boström, who was Prime Minister at the time, fell off his chair. His successor, more sober and with a cooler head than people were looking for at the time, was scolded and he also fell off his chair. Then a grandson's daughter's son of old Jean Baptiste ascended Harald Hårfager's throne, with the stage name of Hakon VII.

*

Arvid lived very happily with his wife. At times, however, he felt a nagging uneasiness about the future. He decided, therefore, that for the time being he would not bring any more children into the world. He remembered with great horror a story from the Acts of the Apostles about a man 'with four unmarried daughters who prophesied'. It was true, his father-in-law Jakob Randel was still managing, but no one could say by what means, much less for how long... One day Arvid met Freutiger on the street. They hadn't seen one another for a long time. Arvid felt a bit embarrassed about his five hundred crown debt. And he asked whether his father-in-law had said anything about it.

'Well, yes,' answered Freutiger, 'he did, actually. I met him at a meeting of the Brotherhood. And he said to me: "Stjärnblom owes you five hundred crowns, doesn't he?" "Oh," I said, "it isn't worth talking about!" "No," said Randel, "I agree!" So we didn't talk about it any more. But a little later that evening he persuaded me to buy shares in "The Svea Palace" for ten thousand crowns. I can hardly remember how that happened. I'm afraid that it will turn out to be waste paper. But his reasons seemed to be so eloquent and beautiful and patriotic.'

At times Arvid felt somewhat uneasy about the future. His wife, however, was a sensible and practical and thrifty woman, and they did manage quite well for the time being. He had seen through her little stratagem about the 'secret engagement' a long time ago and had both forgiven and admired her – it was so simple and brilliant at the same time. Since she had achieved her goal, that is, to get a man, she now paid very little attention to him. And that discovery pleased him:

This, he decided, might really turn out to be a happy marriage for once.

There were small matters that could sometimes irritate him. As the wife of a journalist she considered herself able to understand what his job required him to pretend to understand. Furthermore, she expressed her opinions at social occasions – those few they were not entirely able to avoid – with the greatest of confidence on all that had to do with literature, art and music. And she sang. She had a good, strong voice, but she didn't always carry a tune. He was obliged to accompany her.

One evening they had come home from a party. She was in a bad mood. She had sung, but not been very successful.

'You didn't follow me in your accompaniment,' she said.

'It wasn't that easy, you know,' he answered. 'The human voice – at least your voice – can sing in whatever key; it can sing in a key halfway between C major and D flat. The piano cannot do that! You start in C major and three seconds later you're singing in something between C major and D flat. But the piano isn't able to do that! Therefore, the pianist cannot "follow" you!'

After an evening like that, he would sometimes sit upright in bed and stare sleeplessly into the dark, whispering to himself: 'If only I were alone! If only I were free!

Otherwise, they lived together very happily.

And the years went by.

Arvid walked back and forth through the rooms in the small flat on Kungstensgatan. Finally he stopped in front of a mirror and knotted his white scarf. Dagmar was ready. It was one of her merits that she was always ready in good time when they went out. They were to have dinner at Consul-General Rubin's. It was a day at the beginning of December 1907.

'Let me see,' Dagmar said, 'did you forget your ring?'

Arvid looked for it but could not find it. It was completely inexplicable He must have mislaid it in some strange place. They looked everywhere, but the ring was gone.

The taxi was waiting outside.

'We can't be late at Rubin's,' said Dagmar. 'You'll just have to be without a ring for once. It'll most likely turn up later…'

They rode in silence through the gloomy December darkness.

'Do you think the King is going to die?' Dagmar asked.

The old King was dying.

'It looks that way,' Arvid answered.

Light from the lamps and the shops rushed by the taxi windows like fireflies…

Consul-General Rubin's flat on Sturegatan – the 'real' part of Sturegatan, near Humlegården, was radiant with illumination. One servant and two pretty young girls were walking around with trays of caviar and goose liver canapés and Lysholm's aquavit. The Consul-General was one of the few Swedes who had enough moral courage to offer his guests Norwegian brandy after 1905. He walked among the gentlemen, distributing pieces of paper with the names of dinner partners and a seating plan. On Arvid's card it said: Miss Märta Brehm. He offered his arm to a slender lady with a pale, finely featured, somewhat sad face and, while the little string orchestra played 'Entrance to the Hall of Songs', they marched into the dining room.

Arvid looked around the table. The host had taken Miss Ellen Hej to the table. She resembled an aged and weather-beaten Madonna. The hostess's cavalier was P. A. von Gurkblad. Which was very suitable: she belonged to the old Caroline nobility, born Grothusen... From diagonally across the table he saw Freutiger nodding at him, and he nodded back. Freutiger had Dagmar as his partner. Far away, at the other end of the table, he glimpsed Markel's ravaged face with its drooping mustache, which was starting to become slightly grizzled... Not far from him he saw Henrik Rissler's clownish profile sticking out... and Miss Elga Grothusen, the young, beautiful, celebrated and slandered writer, a niece of Mrs Rubin.

While the soup – *potage au chasseur* – was being served, the orchestra played a minuet from *Don Juan*.

Arvid raised his glass of red wine to his partner, Miss Märta Brehm. She raised hers, lowering her face a little.

What was he supposed to talk with her about? He knew her history, or thought he did. A love story, and a child...he couldn't immediately remember where and from whom he had heard it. But he remembered something about a love affair in her youth with a young medical student who later developed more serious ideas...and was now a seamen's chaplain in Hamburg. Therefore, he could talk with her about anything, except young medical students, illegitimate children, or seamen's chaplains...

'Is Miss Brehm related to the famous author of *The Life of Animals*?' he asked.

'No...'

Arvid felt himself blush. Today I'm having one of my idiot days, he decided. Which is what I always have at big dinner parties. I don't understand why people invite me. I'm not a very entertaining dinner guest, after all.

But Miss Brehm helped him:

'Tell me,' she said, 'are you acquainted with Henrik Rissler?'

'No, not very well. We have met a few times at the newspaper.'

'When I see him,' said Miss Brehm, 'I find it so difficult to see any connection between him and his books.'

'That was actually my first impression of him as well, now that you mention it. But he hasn't ever pretended to be one of his fictional characters.'

'But still... His books are so melancholy, and he himself is always lively and happy, at least he's been so on those occasions when I have met him...'

Arvid thought about it for a while.

'Yes,' he said. 'Maybe you're right. Perhaps the reason is that he doesn't like working. Perhaps that's why he sees everything so black, whenever he sees the need to practice his profession. As soon as he's finished with something, preferably something really dismal and sad, he immediately becomes happy and lively again!'

Miss Brehm was thoughtful.

'Do you really think that that's the way a writer looks inside?' she said

'Well, perhaps...I don't know...since I'm not a writer.'

They were now eating the fish course. It was *trout au gratin*. Schubert 's 'Trout Quintet' was playing.

On Arvid's left side sat the very charming Baroness Freutiger. Freutiger had married a couple of years earlier.

From diagonally across the table he heard Dagmar ask Freutiger:

'Is the baron a very jealous person?'

The question was really somewhat indiscreet, but the Baron answered undaunted:

'Terribly. One time, many years ago, I was engaged to a girl whom I suspected to be a little loose, you know. At first it was only a suspicion and I didn't really know what to think. But one day in April I was walking up Karlavägen. Suddenly I saw my fiancée coming from Nybrogatan, turning the corner without seeing me and continuing on Karlavägen, some distance in front of me. My first idea was, of course, to catch up with her; but then it occurred to me: it might be fun to see where she was going. She entered a doorway! I started to see red! In that particular house there lived one of the people I had suspected of having a fling with her – a lieutenant, and one of my friends, by the way. He had a bachelor's two-room flat on the first floor – both rooms with windows opening on to the street – I'd been there many times and knew exactly the location of every piece of furniture. I stopped and at first didn't know what to do – I didn't want to walk by his windows, perhaps be seen by the two inside and then be laughed at. But I did want to see if the blinds were down. So I had an idea. A streetcar came by, I jumped on it and saw in passing that the bedroom blind had been lowered! Now I knew what to do. I got off the streetcar. Looked at my watch. Only four minutes had passed since she had walked through the door. Too early, I decided. Patience for two, three more minutes. As luck would have it I met an acquaintance, a hack – hmm, excuse me, a journalist – I stopped him and said: "You're going to be my witness now and you'll get material for a funny article for your paper." He looked a little surprised, but I pulled him with me to the window with the lowered blind, pulled off my coat and wrapped it around my hand and arm then punched in the window – pang! – and immediately inserted the other arm and pulled up the blind! I'm not going to try to describe the sight which...etc. There was a crowd, police, a large procession to the nearest police station! The story cost me a one hundred and fifty-crown fine, but I now knew for sure, and I invited the hack – that is the journalist – and a few others to a very big dinner with lots to drink!'

There was a moment of respectful silence among the ladies in Freutiger's vicinity.

'May I ask,' Arvid had turned to the lady on his left, 'what sort of moral the baroness can conclude from this story?'

The baroness answered, with her eyes half-closed and a dry smile:

'That one should stay virtuous – on the first floor...'

The Venetian waltz from *The Tales of Hoffman* was playing.

'Tell me, Mr Stjärnblom,' asked Miss Brehm, 'is it on principle that you don't wear your wedding ring?'

'No,' answered Arvid. 'As a matter of principle I do nothing "on principle". I simply forgot it.'

'Is it possible to forget something like that?' she asked.

'I suppose you can forget just about anything,' he replied.

He looked at her furtively. Only now did he really see her. Her small, fine profile under the curly, brown hair. Her lowered eyes. Her red mouth greedily sucking on an asparagus tip. Her charming small breasts, which quivered in her décolletage. How old could she be? About thirty, perhaps. That sounds bad when referring to a 'miss', he thought, but in reality it isn't so bad at all... Actually, she was more like a young widow or a divorced woman... Suddenly it became clear to him from whom he had heard her 'story': it was Dagmar. No, the very first time he had heard it, it was Freutiger who had told him, at the Rydberg café on Gustav Adolf Square, very briefly and summarily, that she had a child with some chap. But Dagmar had told him the story in greater detail. Märta Brehm had been one of her childhood friends.

'Skoal, Arvid!' Freutiger shouted. 'Why did you put your ring in your waistcoat pocket?'

Arvid turned both waistcoat pockets inside out:

'I haven't put it in my waistcoat pocket,' he said. 'I've forgotten...misplaced it...'

'Yes,' said Dagmar, 'that really is true. He's not the kind who would put his ring in his waistcoat pocket when it suits him. Skoal, Arvid!'

'Skoal, dear Dagmar!'

They trusted each other completely in their marriage. There

were never any jealous scenes. She could not for a moment imagine the slightest possibility of him being in love with another when he had her. And, for a somewhat different reason, he was never jealous of her.

'I am going to make a little confession, Mr Stjärnblom,' Miss Brehm said. 'I have some short stories lying in a desk drawer. I don't know if they are worth anything, but I'd like so much to see them printed. If I were to send them to the *Nationalblad*, who would be the person to judge them and decide whether they are published in the paper or not?'

'That would be Torsten Hedman,' Arvid answered. 'He's in Greece just now, and I don't know when he'll be back. In his absence, however, it's my job, among many others, to read and judge the literary manuscripts that are sent in.'

'In that case, do you think that you might look favourably upon my little efforts?' asked Miss Brehm.

'Without a doubt,' he answered.

He didn't quite know whether he imagined it or not, but under the table he thought he felt his right foot being caressed by a small woman's foot. He made an effort to return the courtesy as tactfully as possible, while they were both staring straight ahead with a dreamlike expression on their faces...

They had reached the poultry course: Snipe. Chopin's 'Funeral March' was playing.

It was strangely quiet around the table.

'Our friend Rubin has bizarre ideas at times,' Freutiger whispered

The servant went around on tiptoe and served an old château wine.

'I love Chopin's "Funeral March",' said Miss Brehm.

'Yes,' answered Arvid. 'However, it was composed for piano, with all the effects calculated for a piano technique. Something is always lost when it is transposed for string instruments.'

'That's true. After all, you are a music critic...'

'Yes, unfortunately. For that reason I will have to leave shortly, just when everything is so pleasant. Mrs Klarholm-Fibiger will be singing Senta in *The Flying Dutchman*, it's the first time she's singing one of the greater Wagnerian roles, and I have promised her not to let it pass unnoted... However, I don't have to be at the Opera until about nine, for the second act.

The 'Funeral March' had ended, and the noise of the conversations was rising again. Arvid once more experienced strange feelings in his right foot, feelings that rose to the more central areas of his nervous system... And he thought: they must be horrible rubbish, those short stories of hers.

P. A. von Gurkblad expressed with a few elegant words the gratitude of the guests. They arose, some with difficulty, and accompanied the ladies to the 'grand salon'.

The gentlemen assembled, as though according to a law of nature, around the Consul-General's cigar boxes: long, thin Manuel Garcia, middle sized, more fully flavored Uppman and small, dainty Henry Clay. And for the guests who neither liked nor tolerated Havana cigars, there were some excellent cheroots.

Arvid took a Manuel Garcia. He calculated that he would be able to smoke about a third of it before leaving for the Opera. Suddenly he found himself standing in the middle of a group with Miss Hej, Henrik Rissler, Markel, Miss Brehm and others. Markel had a Manuel Garcia as well.

'My dear Miss Hej,' he heard Rissler say, 'at the table you asked me why I didn't want to write about your and Mayor Hindlagen's peace address of 1905, and my answer most likely was drowned out in the din. I realized that you hadn't heard it. Well, I had two good reasons. I am neither interested in war, nor am I bloodthirsty; but first of all, I am known as an immoral writer – that is my only principle, and that isn't apt to give me any authority in questions dealing with serious matters – relatively serious matters. On the other hand, however...'

'My dear Hank Rissler,' Miss Hej was all sunshine, 'an

"immoral writer", whatever do you mean by that? Are there not situations where everyone must take part, when the outcome is so important?'

'On the other hand, however,' Rissler continued, 'there are situations in which a people ought to give unlimited authority to those who have power and responsibility. As the Norwegians did in 1905: that was their strength. For that reason, I did not want to be part of something that, even in the most insignificant way, could be used right from the beginning to give our politicians fewer possibilities at the negotiations. It was my honest opinion, as it is now, that a war between Sweden and Norway would have been "the beginning of the end" for the history of both countries...or at least, it would have been the beginning of long hard times in the history of both peoples... But I did not consider myself to be the right person to step forward and inform the leaders of something so obvious. I felt it best to trust that they understood it just as I did. And they seem to have done so!'

'I really thought that you, Rissler, didn't pay attention to politics,' said Märta Brehm.

Rissler didn't get a chance to answer – Markel replied:

'My dear Miss Brehm, don't you know that Hank Rissler was almost arrested a few years ago for provoking an uprising?'

'You always did exaggerate,' said Rissler.

'No, it's completely true. It was election night a couple of years ago. Rissler and I and a couple of others came out of the Rydberg, late at night. Gustav Adolf Square was packed with people who were cheering the latest results. Suddenly, Rissler had the bright idea that he would put himself at the head of the crowd and walk down to the *Aftonpost* and laugh! The *Aftonpost* had, as usual, tried a little last minute gerrymandering and failed, as usual. Fine. Rissler stood on Gustav Adolf Square and yelled as loud as he could: "Now, let's go to the Aftonpost and laugh!" After he had repeated that a few times, the crowd really started moving, and they walked down Fredsgatan, past the Academy of Arts, down to the *Aftonpost,* and there Rissler yelled, with his cane waving in the air like a conductor's baton: Ha, ha, ha! Ha, ha, ha! And the crowd joined him: Ha, ha, ha! Ha, ha, ha! And during a short interval he said to me: "Just think if I were to be arrested for provoking an uprising?" "You will most likely be arrested," I answered, "but you won't be charged with provoking an uprising, but with drunkenness and disorderly conduct instead." At that he paled and sneaked cravenly away through a back street, while the crowd continued to yell Ha ha ha! until the police came and dispersed it...'

'My dear Markel,' said Henrik Rissler, 'what a poet I would be if I could lie as well as you!'

Arvid looked at his Manuel Garcia. He had smoked about a third of it and it was past half past eight. He had to leave and go to the Opera. He expected to have his review written by midnight. At that time he could hail a taxi, pick up Dagmar and drive home.

As he stood in the hallway getting into his overcoat he saw Miss Brehm's fine little head in the crack between two curtains of a doorway.

'Do you have to leave already?' she asked.

'Yes,' he said.

She let go of the curtain and came to him:

'And you won't forget what you promised me?'

He looked at her enquiringly.

'What I promised you?' he asked.

'To help me get my little short stories into your paper.'

He couldn't at that moment remember what he had promised. But she was very sweet, standing there, close to him, with her fine little head bent like a repentant Magdalene. Why on earth should she be repentant? Looking around hastily to reassure himself that no one saw them, he took the little head with both his hands and bent it further still and kissed her somewhere on her spine. Then he lifted her head again, kissed her mouth and said: 'See you!' And left.

There was wet snow falling that evening in December. It would take ten minutes to walk to the Opera. Should he take a cab? An unnecessary expense...

He walked, thinking about Märta Brehm. And about Dagmar.

Why shouldn't I, for once in my life, allow myself a little love affair? After all, you only live once. Dagmar is perfectly fine, but it's a little boring having the same woman day in, day out, night in, night out, year after year. We've been married for almost four years, and I have, literally, never been unfaithful. But...but I don't love her! Why shouldn't I, like others, have room for a love affair in my poor little life? I remember that once, when I was very young, I dreamed about establishing my name, becoming part of Swedish history. That sort of thing certainly doesn't look very likely now. So, why shouldn't I take satisfaction from what is offered? Nonsense. Dagmar is really good enough for me. She sees to it that the curtains of our home are a pure snow-white. I should do that too. And Miss Brehm...she wants her stories in the paper, and for that reason I got a kiss in advance thanks to Torsten Hedman's absence in Greece – if he'd been here he would have received it...could the seed for a *grande passion* really exist in such a beginning? Well, he who lives will see... He could still feel her pointed little tongue moving like a flame...

From the pavement in front of the Opera House he could see, in the distance, dense crowds of people outside the news offices. He met an acquaintance, a journalist, and he stopped him and asked:

'Is the King dead?

'Not yet.'

He went into the Opera. He had calculated his time correctly: the first intermission was almost over when he entered the auditorium and sat down in his usual seat. The public had started to stream in. A short bald gentleman with his wife – a tall, slender and dark already slightly grizzled lady – pushed their way past him, to their parquet seats further in. Arvid had seen her before and knew her by name. She was the lady for whose sake Markel had once, before the turn of the century, spent some time in a mental hospital. He knew that she had seen something no other living human being had ever seen: she had seen Markel crying. In those days she was known as a 'woman of easy virtue'.

The auditorium was now almost completely full.

All around him there was murmuring and talking: so and so is going to divorce his wife and marry so and so… Yes, it's just about certain, I have it from the closest source…

To his right there were still two empty seats. Two ladies slid in at the last minute and sat down at the same moment the lights were turned down.

Lydia.

No? Oh, yes. It was Lydia who was sitting next to him. Very close to him. He had recognized her immediately. Their eyes found each other in the half-dark and made contact during a protracted second. Then she turned her small head away again and seemed to listen to the music, her eyes half closed.

Mrs Klarholm-Fibiger's great and beautiful voice filled the room.

Lydia sat slightly forward, her chin supported by her left hand. Furtively, Arvid looked at that small hand. He saw, right away, that she was not wearing any plain gold rings but only a platinum one with an emerald between two small diamonds. Well, that didn't really have to mean anything, but still… He knew that her husband had bought a property in Södermanland some time after the wedding, and, for all he knew, she had lived a quiet life there ever since with her little girl and her husband whom she honoured and obeyed and perhaps even liked. For there have been examples, it does happen, that an older man wins the love of a young woman. Even if it is nonsense nine times out of ten and there's really something entirely different behind it... She also had a pearl necklace, after all, with an emerald clasp...just as it should be! The rewards of love!

He suddenly felt himself blushing with shame in the dark. Here he sat, next to the love of his youth. For the first time in almost ten years. All he had needed was an emerald clasp to lead him into low and cynical thoughts and fantasies about her... He asked himself: who am I and what am I on my way to becoming? Haven't I sold myself to Dagmar for two thousand a year? Well, actually, that's not the way it happened, but that's certainly what it looks like from the outside... Couldn't Lydia's case be the same? Couldn't it also have happened in a way that is different from how it looks from the outside?

He looked at her furtively. Oh God, how beautiful she was! She had changed in a way he could not explain... She was the same, and yet different. She looked more beautiful than ever, but in a dangerous and forbidding way. There was something strange about her. There was something inside him that said: 'Be careful with this stranger!' Leave this place, go to your office, write your review, get a car and pick up your Dagmar at Rubin's and drive home!

But he didn't get up

Another interval. He heard her exchange a couple of words with her companion, whoever she was. The lady got up and went out. Lydia remained.

Arvid, too, remained where he was. The seats around them had emptied.

Their hands searched for and found each other.

They were silent. Then she said in a low voice:

'Are you happy?'

He was silent for a moment.

'I suppose no one is really happy,' he answered. 'But you have to go on living anyway, as well as you can.'

'Yes,' she said. 'Yes, I suppose you do.'

Her companion returned.
They said no more.

After the theatre he went to his office and, in great haste, wrote a short review, full of warm praise about Klarholm-Fibiger's Senta. After that he hailed a cab and picked up Dagmar at Rubin's. They were just having a lively discussion concerning the racial origins of the royal family. Freutiger argued that they were Jews.

'They are not Jews,' said Markel. 'You've never seen Jews that tall! If anything, they might be Arabs. There is a strong Moorish-Arab mix in the population of Béarn. But then again, what difference does it make? I see no shame in belonging to the race that discovered both God and numbers!

'I am somewhat of a Jew myself, for that matter,' said Markel. 'I'm an eighth of a Jew. My grandmother on my mother's side was half Jewish; her father was a Jew. Apparently he went over to evangelism for one simple reason: what the hell is the point of being a Jew and paying taxes for two religions when you don't believe in any?'

Arvid escorted Dagmar to the car, and they went home.

While she was getting undressed he found a little whisky and soda in the pantry. He made himself a drink and walked back and forth in his study, smoking a cigar. Two, three steps forward, two, three back. He was mumbling a few lines from Viktor Rydberg.

But one whose heart a wood-fairy stole
Has no heart left for a woman,
The dreams in the moonlight own his soul,
He'll love no wife that is human…

Dagmar came in, dressed in her nightgown:
'Here's your ring,' she said. 'I found it in my bed!'

'Oh,' he said.

He continued to pace back and forth.

And if there were aught could ease him,
'Twould be that death would release him...

Again he heard Dagmar's voice:

'Aren't you coming?'

He had stopped in front of his desk. The lid was down. Distractedly, he pulled out the little drawer where the old pencil drawing lay among a lot of other old stuff. The one with the skeletal willows and the migrating birds in formation under heavy autumn clouds. He turned the page: 'I want to go away, oh so far, far away.' That was written furthest up, at the edge. And under it he had himself – he didn't exactly remember when – written these four lines:

Naked autumn willows reflected in calm grey water,
heavy clouds course across the sky, birds flying south.
Tears veil my sight, seeing this yellowed leaf
I once received in a letter. Autumn has reigned here ever since.

Absentmindedly he put the piece of paper into his notebook, as he used to do.

The next morning he woke to the deep and distant ringing of all the city's church bells.

He sat up in bed:

'Now he's dead, the old King,' he said to his sleeping wife. 'The old gentleman who has been King of this country all our lives…'

He went to the window and parted the curtains. It was a sombre, grey, foggy day. From the Institute of Technology across the street an old and dirty flag fluttered at half-mast. The church bells thundered and sang.

There was a fire crackling in his study. He sat at his desk and had just lit his first cigar after breakfast. Dagmar was still asleep. Augusta, the maid, came in with a letter.

He recognized Lydia's handwriting immediately, and tore the envelope open.

Arvid, I'm writing this in my room at the Hotel Continental. I have just returned from the Opera. The desk clerk told me that it would reach you tomorrow morning. If you would like to meet me for a short while on Sunday – I'll be going home to Stjärnvik Monday morning, have been in Stockholm for a few days only to do my Christmas shopping – I'll be having a cup of tea in the dining room at about two thirty. I am alone. And there are almost no guests at that time.

I have no words for what I felt yesterday evening…after so many years…

Lydia.

P.S. Burn this letter.

Thoughts raced through his head. '…home to Stjärnvik…' Since last night he had nursed a vague and secret hope that she perhaps no longer lived with her husband, and that she actually lived in Stockholm… But 'home to Stjärnvik…'

He threw the letter into the fire. It flared up, then curled and turned black.

'Shall I meet her or shall I not?'

He took a two-crown coin out of his wallet.

'Chance will have to decide. Heads I go, tails I don't.'

He spun the coin on his desk top. Tails. Again! Tails.

'Very well, all good things come in threes! Tails.

He was annoyed, more with himself than with the stubborn coin.

'This is childish! Of course I'll go.'

A heavy, brownish-grey fog enveloped the city. At noon it was still almost dark. Sunday people walked by silently as in a funeral procession. The row of poplars in front of the Institute of Technology stood at attention like a ghostly guard of honour. Kungsbacken, from which on beautiful days the view of the city is so bewitching, with its three church steeples and Drottninggatan as a backdrop, was terrible that day. The 'haunted castle' looked gloomier than usual. The heavy mass of the Academy of Natural Sciences seemed deep in sleep. Drottninggatan was black and grey. There was an atmosphere of tomb-like silence despite the tolling of the church bells.

He walked to his office. He now had Torsten Hedman's room to himself. Hedman was mostly away on trips, and Henrik Rissler, who for the time being had taken over his old job as theatre critic, rarely if ever did his work at the office. Instead, he jotted down his short and disparaging reviews with indelible pencil sitting at his table at the Rydberg. A few weeks ago, Stjärnblom had been appointed to take care of foreign affairs in addition to music. He had well-founded hopes of a job as 'Foreign Minister' in the New Year. Unfortunately, however, nothing much was happening out in the world. Just repercussions from the Eulenburg affair and the Moltke-Harden case. He found a copy of *Zukunft* and leafed through it. There was an article in it by Harden that interested him. He sat down at the typewriter and started to translate it.

He was almost finished when a copy boy came in and announced that a lady wanted to see him.

'Ask her to come in...'

It was Miss Brehm. At first he had thought: it is Lydia, but why on earth is she coming here when she has arranged to meet me at the Continental...? He had completely forgotten about Miss Brehm.

'What can I do for you?' he said, and then added immediately: 'Oh, that's right...those short stories... Do you have them with you?'

She started. She seemed nervous and confused.

'Yes,' she said. 'I've brought three of them. But if it's any trouble for you...'

'No, please excuse me,' he said, 'I was working – in the middle of something, a little absentminded, I suppose... It will be a pleasure to read them, and I'll let you know tomorrow or the day after.'

'Thank you so much,' she said. 'Goodbye!'

And with a slight nod of her head, she left.

Thinking about what had happened yesterday, Arvid felt somewhat ashamed of the blunt and abrupt way he had received her, and decided to read her stories with as positive an attitude as possible. As soon as he was finished with the Harden article and had added an explanatory introduction as well as a couple of short comments at the end, he began to read them. The first one was not especially good. However, considering all the junk a large newspaper was forced to use in order to fill up its columns, it could do at a pinch. The second one was completely impossible. But when he read the third story, he was pleasantly surprised to find that it was really good. He immediately initialled it and sent it down to the printers. Then he sat down again and wrote her a letter:

Dear Märta Brehm,

I shall express my opinions of your three stories in the order I happened to read them. 'The Old Cottage' is usable, but no more than that. 'Moonlit Night' is not usable, at least for the Nationalblad. *On the other hand, 'The Red Sofa' shows, according to my modest opinion, real literary talent. It is so good that you can very well attach your name to it, if you wish.*
For the Nationalblad.

Sincerely,
A. Stjärnblom.

He looked at the clock. It was ten past two. Twenty minutes. In twenty minutes he would be sitting with Lydia in the dining room of the Contintenal.

Markel came in:

'No, really,' he said, 'listen to this, Arvid – I just can't stand it any more! There's this skinny, pale old man sitting in the waiting room to see Doncker. The waiting room attendant says to him: "Dr Doncker is busy." "Well, then I'll wait," the old man says. Lundqvist, the editorial secretary, walks by. The old man asks: "Is Dr Doncker here?" "He's busy," Lundqvist tells him. Three or four of our younger staff walk by, and the old man asks each of them: "Is Dr Doncker in?" And all of them answer: "Dr Doncker is busy!" Just now, quite by chance, I found out that Doncker actually went to Berlin a week ago and hasn't returned yet. So he's been gone from the paper for about eight, ten days, and not a soul from the waiting room attendant to me has been aware of his absence!'

'That's quite an accomplishment.'

Markel picked up a proof and glanced through it.

'What on earth is this?' he said. 'Anton Ryge has written a dialogue where one of the people refers to the Gustav Vasa Church as "The Church of Oden". The proofreader has apparently decided that it was a factual mistake and corrected it to Gustav Vasa Church! That reminds me of something that once happened to Gunnar Heiberg with an article for *Verdens Gang*. He had studied the strange expressions on people's faces when they came out of church "especially when they had swallowed their god," he had remarked. The proofreader changed it to "hallowed their god". He corrected it and asked for a new proof. Again, they had set "hallowed their god". So Heiberg went to the chief editor: "This is ridiculous," he said. "There must be a couple of complete idiots doing the proofreading! People hallow their god whenever they go to church, but they certainly don't swallow him every time!" "Don't worry, I'll take care of it," the chief editor said. "I'll see to it that it'll say 'swallowed their god'." Heiberg went home. And in next morning's paper it said: "hallowed their god".'

Arvid walked across Klara's Churchyard. A few streetlights could be seen flickering through the drizzle. He was a few minutes early, so he didn't take the shortcut by way of Klara Vattugränd. He stopped for a moment in front of Bellman's grave. Rain dripped slowly from its two small skeletal trees.

The church bells thundered and sang.

He walked to Klarabergsgatan, turned the corner, walked into the Hotel Continental, left his hat, coat and cane with the porter, took a few steps into the dining room and looked around. It was almost empty. Two gentlemen were sitting at a window table. Otherwise there was no one: the room was half dark, lit only by two or three light bulbs. Lunch was over and it was a long time before dinner. Arvid went all the way to the back of the room and ordered a cup of tea. He hadn't finished ordering when Lydia arrived:

'Make it two,' he said, 'and some toast and butter.'

The waiter turned on the light and disappeared with silent steps across the thickly carpeted floor.

They had hastily and formally shaken hands. He hardly dared look at her.

She had the day's *Nationalblad* with her. She unfolded it and pointed to his review of Mrs Klarholm-Fibiger as Senta in last night's *Flying Dutchman*:

'Did she make that much of an impression on you?' Lydia asked.

'I don't remember,' he said. 'What did I write?'

He read: 'Mrs Klarholm-Fibiger's voice is the sort that awakens dreams and illusions about a happiness that is beyond all that is humanly possible, beyond all that is possible on earth – dreams and illusions of a sensuality over all sensualities, of bliss, of eternal bliss…'

'Well,' he said. 'Did I really write that last night? It must have been because I sat next to you. For the first time in almost ten years, I sat next to you.'

The waiter arrived with the tea and toast and butter.

She said:

'Arvid…?'

He said:

'Lydia…?'

She said:

'Do you love your wife?'

After a moment's thought, he answered:

'I love her in the Lutheran sense.'

'What does that mean?'

'Oh, it doesn't matter…'

They sat in silence and sipped their tea. He was thinking: is she the same as before? The same Lydia I kissed in the lilac arbour more than ten years ago? Do I still love her? Can I love her now that she has given herself to another man? Or perhaps several…

He said:

'Lydia. Do you remember that time almost ten years ago – when you came to Torsten Hedman's room in the editorial office?'

'Yes, I remember… Not very clearly. But I do remember.'

'Do you remember I asked you something, and do you remember what you replied?'

'Yes… No…!'

'I asked you about something. I asked you for something. And you answered: "I want to! But I don't dare!"'

She said, with a veiled smile:

'Did I really say that?'

'Yes.'

'I see… Well, that was then…'

It took him a while to come out with what he wanted to say:

'Have you perhaps become a little more daring since then?'

He tried to meet her eyes, but she looked straight out into the half darkness of the room, and with the same veiled smile she answered:

'Perhaps I have.'

Her answer awakened in him feelings of both terrible anxiety and overwhelming longing.

They were both silent.

Then she said:

'Can you tell me something? Where is Taunitzer Lake?'

'Taunitzer Lake?'

The name sounded familiar, but he couldn't remember just then where he had heard or read about it.

'No,' he said, 'I don't know. I suppose it's somewhere in Germany or Switzerland. But why? Are you planning to go there?'

'I'd like to, very much,' she said. 'If only I could find out where it is.'

'That shouldn't be so difficult.'

'I'm afraid that it might be,' she said. 'I lay awake last night, thinking about a passage in *When We Dead Awaken*. All the time I kept hearing in my head: "Lovely, lovely was life at Taunitzer Lake!" Then I thought: I guess there is no such lake. And perhaps that's just what's so nice about it.'

'Oh, I see... Well, I think you're right. That sort of lake certainly isn't so easy to find on a map.'

They were silent.

She whispered, more to herself than to him:

'After all, you should be allowed, just once in your poor life, to seek your own Taunitzer Lake...'

He caressed her hand.

'Little Lydia,' he murmured, 'little Lydia...' Then he said:

'How are things between you and your husband?'

'Very good,' she answered.

Then she added with a bitter little smile:

'Being with him is so instructive. He knows so much about so many things.'

'I heard about your long honeymoon voyage...'

'Yes. Copenhagen, Hamburg, Bremen, Holland, Belgium, Paris! The Riviera, Milan, Florence, Rome! From Brindisi to Egypt and the pyramids. Three thousand years, or four, or six – I don't remember which – looked down on little Lydia Stille. Then we travelled back by way of Venice, Vienna, Prague, Dresden, Berlin and Trelleborg...'

'But you never saw Taunitzer Lake?'

'No. It isn't listed in the Baedeker.'

They were all alone in the dining room now. The two gentlemen having lunch at the table by the window had left.

Outside the death bells continued their tolling.

He was still holding her left hand in his right.

He raised it and looked at the ring with the emerald.

'That's a beautiful ring,' he said.

'Yes. Markus gave it to me when I said yes.'

He thought for a moment before he said:

'He was so sure of your yes that he bought such an expensive ring beforehand?'

'No, he had it already. He told me a little romantic story about it, which impressed me…at the time… He had had a romance in his youth, something like twenty or thirty years before, and he'd bought the ring for her. But she deceived him, before he had a chance to give it to her. He asked me to promise never to wear it again if I ever deceived him.'

'And have you kept that promise…?'

She looked out into the room and didn't answer.

Then she said:

'I'd like some time to tell you a little about my life. Not now. Later perhaps. Another time. Perhaps best by letter. Winter evenings are long, at home in Stjärnvik. Perhaps I'll make use of them by writing to you from time to time. But you must not answer. He is so jealous and is aware of every letter I get. He doesn't open them. He doesn't ask to read them. But he does notice them.'

'Then you aren't really so very happy with your husband? Little Lydia…?'

'From time to time,' she said, 'we do get to the subject of divorce…winter evenings are so very long! We are always very calm and objective about it, and the final result is always that I stay. He has the upper hand in these discussions. After all, he is my little girl's father. And he has the money.'

Arvid took her hand and passed it over his eyes. There was no one in the room to see it.

A couple of dinner guests arrived and sat down at a table across from them.

He took out his notebook, found the little pencil sketch and placed it in front of her on the table:

Do you remember?' he asked.

She nodded.

'Yes. To think that you've kept it...'

'For many years I've kept it with me, in my notebook.'

She turned the paper over and read the now faded words that she had written and, under them, his four lines of verse. She was silent for a long time, her eyes fixed on nothing.

'And you did get what you wanted?' he asked. 'You went far, far away. But perhaps you long to go even further still?'

She didn't answer, only repeated in a whisper the last words of his verse: 'Autumn has reigned here ever since...'

'When did you write that?' she asked.

'Quite a few years ago. I think it was shortly after my marriage.'

She thought for a while.

'No,' she said, thinking about his question from a minute ago. 'No, I don't want to go further away. I'd like to change that line now. I'd like it to say: "I want to go home, I want to go home, to my real home!" But I simply don't know where that is. I don't know where I belong. I feel as though I am lost. I have sold my soul. The temptation wasn't that small: he took me to the top of the mountain and showed me the whole world! So I became a rich man's poor ornamental wife. Now I know that the words of that song tell the truth: "many years must mend what in a moment broke". Oh, Arvid – that we should have reached the autumn of our lives while still so young!'

He picked up the drawing and put it into his notebook again.

'Yes,' he said. 'Autumn has come too soon for us.'

Little by little more dinner guests arrived, and the room was now fully lit. He called the waiter and paid.

They continued sitting there.

'Autumn has come too early,' he murmured. 'In the end, however, it is up to us whether we want to put up with it or whether we want to make a beautiful summer for ourselves...'

She looked at him with surprise: 'Do you care for me – is it really possible that you still care for me?'

His eyes fastened on hers.

'I can never, never in all eternity care for anyone else so much.'

She had become pale, but her pallor was radiant:

'Is that true?' she asked.

He was too excited to answer. He could feel his throat tightening, that old feeling he hadn't known in almost ten years. But they both continued to sit there and look straight ahead, stiffly and correctly like two mannequins.

'Too much,' he heard her whisper, as in a dream, 'it would be too much for me to go through life without ever having been yours!'

Then, as in a dream, he saw her very calmly pull the emerald ring off her finger and put it into her little purse.

'Come,' she whispered.

He returned to his senses:

'No, no,' he said, 'we can't do it like this. We can't walk up the stairs and through the corridor together. What's your room number?'

'Twelve.'

'First floor?'

'Yes.'

'I'll leave first. I'll go up to the reading room. You stay here a minute or two longer. Then go up to your room. I'll stand in the reading room doorway to see where you go in. Then I'll wait for a moment until there's no one in the corridor, then come to you.'

'Yes, yes.'

He stood in the doorway to the reading room. She came up the stairs and went into her room. There was a maid somewhere at the far end of the corridor. She disappeared into a room.

He stood in her room and turned the key in the lock.

'It would be too much. . . .' he heard her sob, her head against his chest, 'it would be too much. . .'

Outside, the mourning bells were still ringing in the December darkness.

PART IV

'You may love me in the pagan sense!'

Arvid Stjärnblom's hopes for being appointed foreign correspondent for the *Nationalblad* were fulfilled in the new year, 1908. Since he also continued to be music critic, he now earned a little over five thousand crowns a year. And he needed that money. His father-in-law's subsidy had dried up the previous year. Thanks to Dagmar's thriftiness and her sense of order and thanks to a bank loan of two thousand crowns, underwritten by Doncker and Freutiger, they had managed to make ends meet.

Old Jakob Randel kept his affairs going, despite it all. He no longer had his old vigour nor was he as influential. Still, from time to time, especially when he was in a good mood after a good dinner, he'd swear that he would leave at least a hundred thousand to each and every one of his children, whenever it pleased the Lord to call him home. But five minutes later he'd say: 'I'll be damned if I don't go bust next week!' But when 'next week' came round he would give a big dinner, with Cabinet Minister Lundström as showpiece. The cabinet minister had, with surprise and displeasure, witnessed the childish experiment of the first left-wing administration and afterwards resumed his rightful seat at the royal council table.

After just such a dinner, Arvid, emboldened by the wine, had once asked the minister how he felt about women's suffrage.

'Hm-hm,' answered Minister Lundström.

But right away he added, in a more friendly tone:

'Minister, hm-hm....'

Arvid dispensed with trying to find meaning in this oracular answer. Dagmar explained later on, however, that what he had meant was that he should call him 'Uncle' Lundström, just as she did. After all, he was a cousin to her dead mother. Whenever he came for dinner he gave a kind and friendly little speech. This time he had tapped his glass and said:

'Hm-hm. Things have gone up and down in this world for our friend Jakob Randel. Hm-hm. Sometimes up, sometimes down, hm-hm. Right now, it seems to be up, judging from the excellent food and the exquisite wines. Hm-hm. Therefore, I ask the guests to join me in a toast to the host and the hostess! Hm-hm – the hostess and the host, I mean!

Dagmar had been somewhat unhappy at first when her father's contribution had dried up, but he had consoled her as well as he could.

'Dear Dagmar,' he had said, 'when we married, I honestly didn't believe very much in those two thousand a year – at most I thought that we would get them the first year and didn't dare think about a longer time. But now we have had them for three years, and that is very good. I don't have any reason to reproach your father. I had no illusions.'

One day at the beginning of January he received a letter from Lydia – a long letter. They had agreed that she should send it to his office and not his home.

She wrote:

Arvid, in addition to the letter, I am sending you a couple of pages from an old diary. I have never kept a diary regularly for any long periods of time – have only written a few lines once in a while, here and there. You can read the beginning before continuing with the rest of the letter…

He read a small page written in pencil, obviously torn out of a notebook, and numbered with '1' in ink in one corner:

Paris, 23 February '99

I had thought I would keep a diary during my big trip, but up to now I haven't done so.

We arrived in Paris on the evening of the day before yesterday. Yesterday I was at the Luxembourg with Markus and looked for Papa's *Old Pine in the Archipelago*. Of course, I sobbed a bit when I finally found it in an obscure corner.

Today I went to the Louvre. Oh, what can I remember now of all the wonders in those endless galleries…? Yes, I remember one: an old Florentine painting in the Salon carré: *Portrait d'un jeune homme*. By '*Inconnu*', it says in the catalogue 'Unknown master'. But Markus said that it is supposed to be by – what was his name? – Franciabigio, or something like that… I stood in front of the painting for a long time. It made me think of a man

I once knew. Markus saw that it interested me and asked me if I wanted to have a reproduction of it. Yes, I did.

Then we went for a drive in the Bois de Boulogne and had dinner at the Café Anglais together with an old gentleman from the Académie des Inscriptions…

Arvid put down the page and continued with the letter.

You asked me what my life with my husband was like. It isn't very easy to give you an answer. But I'll try.

I suppose that I don't have to tell you that I was not in love with him when we married. He was fifty-one and I was nineteen. That doesn't necessarily mean that he could not win the love of a young woman. He would perhaps have won mine if… Well, that'll come later.

But I did manage to grow to like him very much. Especially during our long wedding voyage. As you know, he is quite a famous archeologist, but despite that he is not at all like a specialist, limited to one subject. Instead, he is knowledgeable about most topics and knows about all kinds of different things; and wherever we went during our voyage he had distinguished acquaintances and friends. And I couldn't help noticing that in every group of people he was always the central figure. I did not love him. But I was more than a little proud to be his little wife: that I can't deny. He led me into a great and new world – new for me…

But…

…But I am a woman, and wanted so much to have a child. And I couldn't keep from becoming aware of the fact that in our conjugal relations (I'm sorry, Arvid, but I have to tell you about this) he always made sure that there would not be a child. Once I asked him: Why do you do this? He answered that he did not want to have children. Why don't you want to have children? I

asked. Because I am a genius. That's between you and me, so don't talk about it; but I am a genius. And geniuses' children are often idiots. That's why I don't want any children. I lay there for a long time and thought about it. And then I said: But it's possible that the child might take after me and I'm not a genius, after all...and so the child doesn't have to be an idiot... That night – it was at a hotel in Venice – I think that night my little Marianne, who is eight and a half years old now, was conceived.

But when I was a few months pregnant – after we had returned home – I became aware of the fact that he had developed an uncontrollable aversion to my condition. I didn't understand it right away. He became more and more irritable and nervous as the days went by – I had never seen him that way before. Day in day out he would remain in his study and take his meals by himself. And when the time came for me to give birth to the child, he went away! There was some library or archive in Berlin where he suddenly needed to do some studies. And he didn't come home until he received the telegram that all had gone well.

I began to wonder. And I don't know whether you can understand how deeply and irreparably injured I felt. I began to suspect that his fear of becoming the father of a backward child was only a pretext. He had bought me to be his legal lover. Pregnancy and children were not part of his programme.

I believe that I can assure you that I went into my marriage with the most genuine desire to keep to all my obligations towards my husband. But after that I no longer felt I had any obligations – none at all. When the temptation came (it was a few years later) and I met a man who wanted me and impressed me in some way, I fell almost immediately.

As you read this now, you are probably thinking about the emerald ring, and wonder whether I have kept my promise not to wear it again after that day. Well, you already know that I didn't. That is one of Markus's favourite ideas: that the truth is harmful and that illusions and mistakes have been the mainspring of everything great that has been achieved in the world and the seed of all that has to do with human happiness. I have turned his own idea upon him and let him continue living with his illusion.

Please, do not ever ask me about the man I loved. Oh, Arvid, do I hurt you by writing the word loved? But I must do it. Because it is true. Or it was true.

I loved you ten years ago, and I love you now. But at that time – a little more than four years ago – you had been out of my life for so long. And I had just read about your engagement in the paper. And I, also, wanted to live just once.

I don't want to say any more about it. Yes, I can say that it didn't last long. One year, approximately.

The other diary page is from when it was over.

He took the page and read:

September, 1904

So, finished. So was that all it was? Nothing else? Nothing more?

Dead leaves whirl around in the wind out there. Dead leaves fall on to garden walks. There are some asters on my table. And a dead leaf dances in through the window and falls down on this page.

Nothing else – nothing more…

He picked up the letter again and read:

And now, Arvid, you are to be my judge. I put my situation in your hands, and you may condemn or acquit me as you think best. I don't want you to write me a letter, only send me some printed matter (a newspaper or whatever) as a sign that you have received my letter. If you condemn me and therefore no longer want to have anything to do with me, place the stamp upside down. But if you acquit me, place it the right way up.

Lydia.

Arvid sat and thought.

Not for a moment, of course, did he think that he would place the stamp upside down. He was thinking about other things.

Markus Roslin. That outstanding archeologist and historian of culture whose works he had read and followed with a layman's admiration...Knight Commander of the North Star, officer in the Legion of Honour, member of the Academy of Sciences and 'one of the eighteen' and so on...and Lydia.

Lydia. The love of my youth. My only love. Who has quite simply made this great scientist a cuckold. And, despite it all, I cannot call him guilty after having read the report...that is to say, I have only got to know one side of it...but the other side I will most likely never know. Men are more silent about such matters.

Is there still a future for the two of us? For Lydia and me? In that case I would first of all have to divorce Dagmar. Oh, it's so easy for rich people! Lydia can, most likely, divorce her husband easily; he is rich. But I? My annual income isn't enough to share... And Dagmar? What should I say to her? That I don't love her? That I've never loved her? It would be the end of the world for her! Should I remind her about our 'promise of freedom'?

The memory of that childish promise made him smile. Once when they were engaged, not long before the wedding, they had given each other the solemn promise that if one of them, one day, wanted to be free, the other would not do anything to prevent it. Actually, it had been she who had asked for that promise – such promises were common in those days and naturally turned out to be meaningless when things became serious.

And Anna Maria and little Astrid – should they grow up without a father? Or would they soon enough get a 'new Papa'...?

No. He pushed away the thought of divorce as something unthinkable. And, after all, Lydia did not say in her letter the least little thing that might indicate that she herself thought about trying to divorce her husband.

He thought again about her letter. He had hardly been

surprised about the fact that she had taken a lover. His instinct had already whispered to him about something of the sort when they were together that December day at the hotel.

'Now, you are to be my judge.' I'm certainly not the right person for that, he decided.

He picked up a French paper that was lying on his desk. Put a label on it with her name and address typed.

And he placed the stamp the right way up.

'You're so silent and sullen today,' Dagmar said at the dinner table. 'Is anything wrong?'

'No,' he said.

After a while he added:

'I'm sitting here thinking that I'll have to learn Russian.'

Up until now he had been able to employ a young man, Kaj Lidner, who came into the editorial office once a day and looked through *Novoje Vremja* to see whether there was anything of importance in it, and, if so, translate it for him

Almost every day now there was a letter from Lydia on his desk when he arrived at the paper.

In one letter she wrote:

Yesterday Markus himself brought up the subject of divorce. He started by saying: 'I think that you are unhappy here. Perhaps you would rather live in Stockholm?' – 'I'd like that very much,' I said. – 'And why is that?' he asked. 'Theatres, society, and such?' – 'Perhaps that too,' I said, 'but that is not what's most important. What's important is that I don't love you, and life with you is a torment for me.' – 'Love,' he twisted out of himself with his fatherly and indulgent smile, which I have learned to hate more than anything else. 'Little Lydia, I will soon be an old man but I am not an idiot. Have I ever even asked whether you "loved" me?' – No, I had to admit that he was right. He's never asked me that. He was too smart for that.

Then he continued, 'We've already talked about divorce a couple of times. I have thought a lot about it and I have a proposition to make to you. I don't want to be parted from our little Marianne; she will stay here. You can have your freedom, and you'll get five thousand a year in support, but with one condition: that you spend three months here every year, two in the summer and one around Christmas and New Year. During those months everything will be the same between us.'

I answered: 'I would be extremely happy were you to give me two thousand a year without any conditions.'

He didn't answer, but went to his room and locked the door. As though he had to worry about my trying to force my way in… Now I believe that I have made my decision. Nevertheless, I am still unsure…

Lydia.

Another letter arrived the following day:

Yes, I have made my decision. No law can force a woman to live together with her husband if she doesn't want to. On the other hand, he has no obligation in such a case to support her. But I have about three thousand in the bank; it is my inheritance from Father. Then I have my jewels. I was given them. They are mine – and I have paid honestly for them, I was about to say… Paid for them with ten of the best years of my youth – isn't that enough? The pearl necklace is surely worth many thousands. So I have enough for several years and, of course, I will try to get some work

One thing, Arvid: I don't want you to take any steps towards a divorce because of me. Just as before I do not want to cause you trouble. You have enough as it is. I will try to forget that you have a wife and children and a whole little world that is not mine. I am sure that we will be able to have moments when both of us forget everything that is not us – the two of us…

Lydia.

And two days later, another letter:

Oh, Arvid, you cannot imagine how radiantly happy I was when I woke up this morning! The branches of the trees in the park were heavy with glistening snow… Sunshine and a high blue sky! Just as I was rolling up the shade there was a bullfinch sitting on a branch close to my window – I thought that I could see its red downy breast panting, I thought I could see its little heart fluttering…

Markus has suddenly changed his mind. We have barely spoken during the past few days, and he has taken all his meals in his room. Yesterday, however, he ate at the dinner table and was kind and nice, which he can be whenever he wants to. After dinner he asked me to play. I played the Pathétique. He sat near the fireplace in a large armchair. Marianne stood at the piano with me. It was half dark in the large room, with only the two lighted candles on the piano and the light from the fire…he asked for more music, I played a couple of Chopin's preludes… Then Marianne went to bed: it was nine o'clock.

We were alone. 'Sit down here,' he told me. I sat down in an armchair next to the fireplace. 'Little Lydia,' he said. 'You will get what you want.' I didn't answer. There was nothing I could say at that point and I wanted to hear whether he had more to say.

He said, 'The way things have become between us most recently, little Lydia – especially during the weeks after your trip to Stockholm before Christmas – I cannot doubt the fact that you have fallen in love with someone. We're not going to say any more about that. The natural consequence of this is that every day and every moment you must wish me dead and buried. Am I wrong? No, you don't have to answer. I don't even indirectly want to be responsible for the fact that perhaps one day a dangerous and criminal thought might enter your dear little head. I have cherished you very much, little Lydia – and I still cherish you very much... And now you will get what you want.'

I found no words. I took his hand and wet it with my kisses and tears. I kissed his white hair. It has turned completely white during this past year.

Then he said, 'It goes without saying that if you at any time feel like coming here to visit your little Marianne and your old home, you will be a very welcome guest...'

With great difficulty I managed to say 'thank you'.

We continued sitting there for a long time, staring into the dying glow of the fire. Then we said goodnight and went each to our own rooms.

Today, after breakfast, we talked about the practical details. He wanted to give me five thousand a year (without conditions). But I kept to my two thousand. I don't want to have more of his money than I need to live on. He said that so little support could cause talk and defamation of all sorts – people will believe that I had violated my marital vows and had therefore been dismissed with a paltry sum... But I kept to my two thousand. I don't care about people's talk. I didn't want to have more than what I feel I have earned – to some extent...and I have never been interested in luxury. A little two-room flat in Stockholm and some furniture for it are all I need, I told him. Then he asked that I at least let him give me money for the furniture. And, for that, I thanked him.

And now it has all been arranged. At the beginning of next week I will take a trip to Copenhagen, together with Ester (Ester Roslin, a relative of Markus's, who is better friends with me than with him – she was the friend I had with me at the Opera), and in two weeks at the latest, I will be free. Free – free!

Lydia.

A week went by. Then a little picture postcard came from Copenhagen with the City Hall tower and the Bristol and a short greeting. After another few days a new letter:

Arvid. Everything has now been arranged. In a few days I shall be in Stockholm. Don't come to meet me at the station, since I will have Ester with me. We have to be very careful – I must be careful about my reputation for the sake of my little girl. Also for Markus's sake; he's been generous and I don't want to cause him trouble unnecessarily. The best thing would be for us not to meet until I have put my new little home in order. It would be best if I could find a two-room flat with gas and water pipes in the hall. But then!

Oh, Arvid, all that longing for real love that has collected inside of me after so many long, empty years is now waiting for you…

Lydia.

Arvid sat there, holding the letter, lost in thought. He suddenly felt so small at the prospect of what was waiting for him. To still such a longing – that was definitely not a small matter…

But it's Lydia. And I love her.

It was a day in March around the time of the Equinox. The day before Annunciation. No newspapers were coming out the following day, and he was free – all day and all night.

In the morning he had received a postcard:

Dear Arvid,

You have, as you will remember, promised to come out to visit me some time and look at my paintings. You are very welcome this evening and I assume you will spend the night – the last train leaves at 11.30, and that's usually the best time of the evening. There'll be a couple of other fellows here too.

Your friend
Hans Bergling.

This postcard was from Lydia. His friend Bergling was as made up as his name. She had, after discussing it with him, written the postcard in a hand she had tried to make large and masculine. He had also seen to it that he mentioned his friend Bergling a few times at home. They had met at the Liberal Club. He was a talented and promising young painter. He lived in the countryside somewhere towards Saltsjöbadet, but he was a bachelor and couldn't invite ladies. Thus, the invitation did not come as a surprise for Dagmar:

'Yes,' she said. 'Good luck and have fun!'

He didn't want to go to Lydia's directly from his dinner table at home. For that reason, under some pretence, he ate dinner by himself at the Continental. He managed to get the same table at which he had sat with Lydia on that December day when the church bells were ringing about the death of the King...

While he was sitting there with his solitary dinner, he was thinking:

I am thirty-three years old, and she is twenty-eight – no, she was twenty-nine a couple of weeks ago… And I love her, and life is wonderful!

He continued:

Despite it all, the day will come when this will be no more than a memory. When I, as an old man, will sit at my fireplace and stare into a dying fire and whisper to myself: 'Lovely, lovely was life at Taunizter Lake!'

But all the same. All the same! Does it really have to be so completely impossible for us to one day be granted a chance to live and age together? Wouldn't it be possible for Dagmar to fall in love with someone and suggest divorce? Oh, illusions! It was, of course, unthinkable for Dagmar to fall in love with someone. He was by no means egocentric enough to think it impossible – but that she would, in such a case, tell him about it and suggest a divorce, that was pretty unthinkable…

Rather, he decided, she would go about it in about the same way I am doing now…

… At ten to six he called a covered cab and went to Lydia's. He did so to avoid meeting acquaintances, or Dagmar, for that matter, on the street…

Lydia had managed to find a two-room flat on Johannesgatan, on the top floor, under the roof. He climbed the four flights of stairs slowly and checked the names on all the doors to find out whether anyone he knew lived there. There were a few families he had heard about, but no one he knew. When he reached the fifth floor Lydia opened the door before he had a chance to ring the bell:

'I was standing at the window and saw when you came,' she whispered.

The two rooms were not large. The bedroom was very small. Each room had only one window, but the view was wide and beautiful from them. An ice-blue evening sky arched high and cold over the red-speckled brick steeple of the church and the naked tree skeletons in the graveyard. Over the roofs of Döbelnsgatan you could see all the way to Kungsholmen.

The outer room, the larger one, she had furnished with mahogany furniture. Her chest of drawers from her childhood home, in the style of Karl Johan, was also there. On the wall over the piano, an old square piano of the sort that one sees less and less and is certainly not made any more, hung a long row of ten or twelve small portraits of great composers in thin black frames: Handel, Beethoven, Schumann, Schubert, Chopin, Wagner, Bizet and finally Grieg and Sjögren. Higher up was a sketch of her father's: the little red fisherman's shack in the archipelago between knotty pines: *Sunshine after the Rain.*

'Shall I light the candles?' she asked.

It was half dark in the room.

'Oh, not yet,' he answered.

She had neither electric light nor kerosene lamps. The apartment was wired, but she didn't like it and hadn't bothered to install any lamps. Kerosene lamps were too dirty and unpleasant. On her desk were two old silver candelabra with three candles each. On the old chest of drawers from her childhood home there were two narrow candlesticks of old 'golden bronze' in front of an Empire mirror. On the piano there were two candles with green silk shades.

'I do think it is getting a bit dark,' she said. 'Can you read what it says in the open book on the piano?'

It was a little song by Tosti: *'Quando cadran le foglie'* – 'When the leaves fall from the trees'.

'Yes,' he said, 'I certainly can…'

'Do you remember?'

Yes. He remembered. He had hummed it for her once, more than ten years ago in a lilac arbour in a little garden.

She sat down at the piano and sang with a thin, clear voice

that was trembling a little with emotion, perhaps:

When the leaves fall from the trees and you visit
my grave, in the holy soil –
far back in the corner stands the little crucifix
and small flowers adorn the green knoll…

If you then pick for your curls
the flowers to which my heart has given birth,
then know that they are songs which I have thought but not writ;
words of love, to you not said.

He stood behind her and caressed her hair. When she had finished singing, he said:

'Yes, I remember. They used to sing this song a lot at that time. I think it was Sven Scholander who had made it popular. You just don't hear it any more.'

They were sitting at the window. It was getting dark. A solitary, dark-purple cloud was moving slowly, high above the top of the church steeple. Down in the city below, the lamps were lit. There were no longer small children playing among the graves in the churchyard. The stars came out one at a time. In the west, Venus twinkled very close to the dark-purple cloud, and in the south, away over Kungsholmen, Mars was shining with its reddish gleam.

She sat there with his right hand between both of hers.

'Tell me something,' she said. 'How did you come to be married?'

He answered, somewhat evasively:

'I suppose it happened the way it usually does. A man needs a woman, and a woman needs a man. She was a beautiful young woman. She still is.'

Lydia was quiet for a long time, looking out into the darkening blue.

'Well, I've never seen her. Is she blonde or dark?'

'Blonde.'

'Oh well, what difference does it make...?'

They were both silent.

'Of course,' she said. 'I've completely forgotten to thank you for what you sent me this morning. But it's standing on a table in the bedroom.'

He had sent her some French pears, some bunches of blue grapes, some chocolate creams and a couple of bottles of Haut-Sauternes. He had first asked her what sort of wine she liked best. She had answered that she didn't really care for wine but, if necessary, she liked Haut-Sauternes best.

They were silent. She held his right hand between her hands. It was getting darker and darker. The red speckled church steeple was black against the cold blue March sky.

She said:

'Do you remember our meeting at the Continental, in December?'

'If I remember...'

'How could I have been so daring? At such a grand and respectable hotel! I must have been absolutely crazy. Someone could have come looking for me. Ester, for example, could have knocked on the door. The door is closed, and no one answers. What would we have done? What would I have done?'

'Well, I don't really know...'

'Oh, Arvid, we have to be terribly careful. We can never again allow ourselves that sort of craziness... You really can't come here so often that people will begin to notice. We will never be able to go out together or even stop and talk for half a minute, if we happen to meet on the street.'

'No, of course...'

They were quiet again. Down below a gas lamp flickered here and there among the old tree skeletons. And up above, in the cold blue, Venus and Mars were burning.

Then she said:

'Do you remember that I asked you, that time at the Continental: do you love your wife?'

'Yes...'

'Do you remember that you answered: I love her in the Lutheran sense?'

'Yes.'

'I asked: what does that mean?'

'Yes,' he said, 'I remember very well. Almost four hundred years ago Martin Luther's view was that real love develops naturally between husband and wife when they act according to the dictates of nature and love. I suppose there is some truth in that, but not much.

Lydia was silent for a long time.

'No,' she whispered, 'not much...'

He said:

'No. It makes one think of the Zinzendorf Brotherhood's method a couple of centuries later: they used to draw lots for wives and husbands. The outcome was considered the will of God. All that had to do with liking and attraction and love came from the devil. Love was, according to Luther, only allowed in marriage. Outside of marriage it wasn't called love but fornication and adultery and all sorts of other ugly things and it was destined for especially high temperatures in hell...

Lydia had suddenly become pale. But her pale face was glowing.

'Come,' she said. 'You may love me in the pagan sense!'

She led him by the hand into the bedroom and lit two candles in front of the mirror.

Two candles. He had a confused idea that they implied some sort of a religious ceremony.

...There were no blinds to let down; she had yet to acquire any. They weren't needed. There were no neighbours to see them. There was only the brick steeple and the old and tall tree skeletons in the churchyard and a dark blue March sky and two big stars. Now the smaller ones were also coming out, one after the other...

Slowly, dreamily, she began to loosen her clothes.

...

A small room with a large bed. Two lighted candles in front of a mirror. And a window on to the stars and infinity.

He said:

'Lydia. I thought about something on my way here.'

'What did you think about...?

'I wondered: is it really completely impossible for you and me to be able to one day live and get old together? Will I be allowed to die with my head resting on your delightful, lovable lap?'

She answered sitting straight up in the bed:

'But you do have a wife, whom you love "in the Lutheran sense".'

He said:

'Perhaps I can be divorced from her some day. It's impossible just now. Her father was rich, but is now ruined and poor. I've told you about it. It would look very bad if I asked for a divorce.'

'Yes, yes,' she said 'I haven't in the slightest way asked you to do that. You're stuck, I'm well aware of that. I will just have to take what I can get. I love you. I haven't made any conditions, you have not taken me "on the promise of marriage"... We simply have to adjust to what we've got... I am glad that I have myself again and my name. That I, once again, have become Lydia Stille. I feel that I have regained something of myself, something that I had lost, thrown away... Did you see my little brass plate on the door? It says *Lydia Stille* on it! Nothing else, nothing else! And nothing else will ever be on my door – neither Roslin nor Stjärnblom nor anything else!

He lay there thinking.

'I'm not that interested in names on doors,' he said, 'but sometimes I dream about a future for the two of us. The two of us together. What I wanted to know was whether you also dream such things. Apparently, you don't.'

She whispered into the night:

'I love you.'

...

They had both slept or dozed when she woke him:

'Are you hungry?' she asked.

'Are you?'

'Yes. I have food.'

She got up and swept a robe around herself.

After a while she had set the table with bread and butter, cold spareribs and more. They still had some of the French pears and blue grapes and the chocolates. They had only emptied one of the bottles of Haut-Sauternes.

'It's only twelve thirty,' she said.

He filled the glasses. They drank to each other merrily:

'Skoal, Hans Bergling!' he said.

She laughed so much she almost choked on her wine.

'When I wrote that postcard,' she said, "Hans Bergling" almost became a living human being for me. I even imagined what he looks like. He's short and squat, he has thick bristly black hair and a greyish-yellow drooping moustache. And his jacket is stained with paint.'

'Shouldn't we also give him a little pointed beard?' Arvid suggested.

'No,' she answered thoughtfully. 'No, that doesn't go with his type at all.'

'By the way,' said Arvid, 'haven't we actually stolen "our friend Bergling" from a novella by Anatole France – Putois?'

'I hadn't thought about that until you mentioned it. It isn't impossible. "Our friend Bergling" really does resemble Putois a little...'

The two candles in front of the mirror had almost burned down. She went to get two new ones, lit them and put out the others.

... And again...

...Her eyes were wide open, their expression grave and firm: her upper lip drawn up a little and her teeth shone in the half dark...

... They both woke up. They sat up straight. Two shadowy faces, which slightly resembled theirs, were staring back at them – they seemed far away, even though the room was so small – out of the mirror with the two candles.

It was nearly five o'clock

'Would you like to sit by the window for a while and look at the stars?' she asked.

She lent him the bathrobe. She swept her evening fur around herself.

There were no more stars – the two large ones had gone down, and the small ones had already become invisible in the paling dawn. In the southwest, very close to the church steeple, they could see the moon's crescent, yellow in the ever-deepening blue.

They sat there, holding hands.

She sat with her head slightly bent forward, watching the blue sky.

She said:

'Just a short while ago the moon was to the left of the steeple. Now it is behind the steeple and in a little while it'll come out again on its right hand side. I've seen this many, many times: the moon moves from left to right. Once, somewhere on the Riviera, I mentioned this to Markus. He said that, in reality, the moon moves from right to left. He explained the whole thing to me, and I think I understood. But I've forgotten it now.'

Arvid thought about it. He had once taken an exam in astronomy at Uppsala and got a B+ in it. However, nature has fortunately endowed human beings with the ability to forget. Otherwise it would be impossible to tolerate living. He thought that he sort of remembered how it worked, but it wasn't easy to explain in a few words.

'It isn't only the moon,' he said, 'that to our eyes moves from left to right in the sky. The sun and all the stars do too. If you look more closely at how the moon moves – not just for a short while like now, but week after week, or even night after night, then you'll see for yourself that it moves from right to left. At this time yesterday it was much further to the right of the church steeple. Tomorrow at this time, it will be quite a distance to the left. Get up at ten minutes to five tomorrow morning and you'll see that it's moved quite a distance from right to left…'

He stopped. He had thought he would give a more detailed explanation, but kept it to himself. He had suddenly remembered the old school principal's friendly words, that he was 'a born teacher'. So he stopped.

They sat cheek to cheek.

'What is happiness?' she whispered.

'Nobody knows,' he answered. 'Or else it is something that you imagine and doesn't exist. Is it actually possible to imagine it? Can you imagine a constant, everlasting happiness – for it has to be everlasting: otherwise it would be poisoned by the thought of its end…after all, your precious stones and your pearls didn't bring you any happiness, did they?'

She smiled dimly.

'No…'

'When the author of the *Book of Revelations* describes eternal bliss, he describes it with the image of a city – he apparently was a city dweller – which is suspended from the sky, a new Jerusalem, where the houses are pure gold, the city wall of jasper and the twelve gates of twelve different sorts of precious and semi-precious stones. That is how inadequate humanity is when it has to imagine the greatest happiness and bliss.'

They were both silent.

'Aren't you cold?' she asked.

'Yes, a little,' he said.

Then they went back to bed again.

The end of March and the beginning of April were so beautiful that spring. There was a mood, something in the air, that reminded him of some spring a long time ago… Perhaps it was that spring day ten years ago when he was walking in Kungsträdgården with Philip Stille, and the late King walked by, and he met Freutiger on Gustav Adolf Square, and they went to the Rydberg together, then read the announcement of an engagement in the *Aftonpost*…

On one of the last days of March, around five o'clock in the afternoon, he was walking up Drottninggatan on his way home. He had just met Lydia – she was walking on the other side of the street, together with Miss Ester – and they had exchanged a somewhat stiff and formal greeting.

He stopped in front of a jeweller's window. In a corner of the window there was a small pin made of silver or platinum with a blood red stone, which looked to him like a ruby. He read the price tag: 18.50. I guess it isn't platinum, he decided – silver, at best. But the stone? It was too cheap to be a ruby and too expensive for a piece of glass. He went inside and asked what sort of a stone it was. 'It is a ruby amalgamate,' came the reply.

He decided to buy it for Dagmar

Poor Dagmar, he was thinking as he walked, poor, dear little Dagmar… She spends her day at home, happy and cheerful and as sure of me as Luther was of the Bible. She neither knows nor suspects nor fears anything at all. I have always believed – well, one knows oneself so poorly – but up to now I have always believed that I was an honest and straightforward person. Without going to extremes, of course: I don't necessarily accost my acquaintances and tell them what I think of them. Anyway, I have always imagined that honesty and a certain disinterested love of truth were two of my most important traits. Now I find myself in situations that make falsehood, trickery and lies almost daily necessities and I realize to my surprise that I have talents in these realms, as well…

Last night he had not come home until six in the morning. He had already phoned Dagmar from his office earlier in the evening to tell her that Hans Bergling was in town and that they would go out to have some drinks. So she knew ahead of time that he wouldn't be coming home too early.

Dagmar was very happy and surprised by his small present.

'Is it a ruby?' she asked.

'No,' he said.

'Is it an imitation then?'

'No, it's half genuine. Chemists have found a way to amalgamate a lot of very small rubies, so small that they have no value as they are. It's called a "ruby amalgamate".'

'How strange!' she said. 'So is it impossible to tell the difference between that and a real ruby?'

'I don't know whether it's impossible, but I wouldn't be able to tell…'

Then they talked about a little of everything. About 'Uncle Lundström' and other relations. Dagmar said:

'It's really very nice to see you in a good mood at last. I suppose you're not aware of how surly and impossible you've been these past few months. Don't you think we should invite your friend Bergling to visit us some time?

'Well – yes – of course, we should perhaps do so…'

But after a while he added:

'Hans Bergling is a very strange individual. He's interested in only two things in this world: paint and drink. When he's had a few, he starts talking philosophy. He's absolutely tormented by the company of women. He doesn't know how to express himself in their presence, doesn't know what kind of language is allowed and what isn't... He's very polite towards ladies; he bows so low that his thick, black hair falls in his eyes and punch or whiskey drips from his little greyish-yellow moustache. As I said, he's a strange individual, and I don't think he'd be very comfortable in our place. Besides, he's suffering from megalomania right now: he's managed to sell a painting to Mr Steel, the bank director. He's represented in the 'Steel gallery'! Which is quite important! I think it would be best for us to wait for him to calm down a bit before inviting him to our simple little home'

'I suppose we'll have to wait then,' said Dagmar.

June blossomed and was delightful.

On the second of the month Arvid rented a car and drove Dagmar, Anna Maria, little Astrid and the maid to Central Station. As usual, they were to spend their summer up in Dalby, at his father's. He would join them later that summer, on his vacation. At least, that's what he had said to Dagmar. He had promised Lydia that he would, of course, find some reason to stay in town.

On the day before Whit Sunday they took a trip to Strängnäs. It was somewhat risky but they were tired of having to be so careful all the time... He had reserved a room at the City Hotel for Mr Bergling, the painter, and his wife. Nevertheless, they almost walked into a very difficult situation. The hotel receptionist greeted them cheerfully:

'Why, it's Mr Stjärnblom!'

Arvid searched his memory frantically and found that the young man had been a former messenger boy who had worked in the *Nationalblad* hallway ten years ago.

'You're Oscar, aren't you?' he said. 'Excuse me, but I've forgotten your last name...'

'Larsson.'

'Of course. Tell me, Mr Larsson, didn't Mr Bergling, the painter, reserve a room here?'

'Yes, that's right...'

'Well, he's asked me to let you know that he was unexpectedly prevented from coming. But we'll be happy to take his room.'

'That's fine...'

At sundown they walked around the small town. The air was

warm and damp. It had rained and cleared up again. There was a wonderful fragrance from the lilac and bird-cherry bushes. The rugged and stern steeple of the old cathedral was dark against the light June sky. The waters of Lake Mälaren were still and reflected the empty blue sky.

The next day, Whit Sunday, they went to church. They joined the others and sang 'Great Is God In His Heaven'. They inclined their heads with the others while confessing their sins. And they listened to the sermon. It was a venerable old pastor – perhaps even the bishop – it being Whit Sunday – who delivered the sermon on the outpouring of the Holy Ghost upon the apostles. He spent a long time talking about the great miracle that took place at that time: when Jesus's apostles, those ignorant and poor men, were granted by the Holy Ghost the gift of mastering all the languages spoken by Parthians and Medes and Elamites and those who lived out in Mesopotamia and Judea and Cappadocia, Pontos and Asia, and Egypt and the Libyan areas near Cyrenaica, and the foreigners from Rome, the Jews and the proselytes, Cretans and Arabs…

Arvid felt Lydia's head sinking quietly on to his shoulder. He was feeling a little sleepy as well. However, he was still able to perceive that the pastor had now started to talk about the modern practice of speaking in tongues:

'We,' he said, 'cannot, as Christians, doubt the power of Almighty God to perform, day after day, the same miracles as then, or even other similar ones. But God does not perform any miracles without a purpose. By the Grace of the Holy Ghost, He granted the apostles the gift to be able to speak to foreign people in order to spread the Word. That was only possible by means of a miracle – a really great and beautiful and meaningful miracle! But if a Swedish man were to preach the Word in a congregation of Swedish men and women and suddenly begin to speak in Mesopotamian, it would certainly be – that is, if it really is Mesopotamian, a language about which the most learned in our time know only very little – a miracle, but one whose meaning is not easy to understand…'

Arvid began to drop off as well… They hadn't slept much that night.

They were awakened by the powerful noise from the organ. Half awake, they joined the others in singing the psalm:

Come, Holy Ghost, God and Lord,
With all your graces now outpoured
On each believer's mind and heart;
Your fervent love to them impart.
Lord, by the brightness of your light
In holy faith your Church unite;
From ev'ry land and ev'ry tongue,
This to your praise, O Lord, our God, be sung.

Come, holy Light, guide divine,
Now cause the Word of life to shine.
Teach us to know our God aright
And call him Father with delight.
From ev'ry error keep us free;
Let none but Christ our master be,
That we in living faith abide,
In Him, our Lord, with all our might confide.

Come, holy Fire, comfort true,
Grant us the will your work to do
And in your service to abide;
Let trials turn us not aside.

After the service they went to look at the tomb of Sten Sture the elder and Bishop Rogge's slippers and some other historical relics. When they came out into the churchyard they sat on a bench in the shade of the old red brick walls of the cathedral. A pauper's funeral, with a young, pale, pimply faced pastor and a few poorly dressed mourners passed by.

And the lake's surface was still and shining and the sky was blue and empty with no showers in sight.

'Tell me,' said Lydia. 'Tell me something about the "Holy Ghost".'

'Well,' said Arvid, 'that's not easy to talk about in a few words. There is a Trinity, comprising father, mother and son, in almost all early religions connected with the creation of what is now called "Christianity". The first Christians were afflicted with a hatred and contempt for women – for reasons I don't remember – and they would not allow a woman to become a god. Otherwise the Virgin Mary, mother of God, would naturally have become a god. But she was a woman and did not count. However, there was supposed to be a Trinity. Therefore, the Holy Ghost was called in to function as a substitute. This was decided at a Church Council. The following is the latest fashionable news from the Kingdom of Heaven: a sinner dies and goes up to the pearly gates and knocks on the door and says to Saint Peter: "Excuse me, I'm actually not supposed to be here, I'm going to the other place; but could you possibly let me take a look through a little hole?" "Yes, of course," says Saint Peter, and he points out the most important people there and says, "That's God the Father sitting there, and there's Jesus," and so on. "But," the sinner, who is supposed to go to the other place, wants to know, "who is that gentleman there, who looks so sad and melancholy?" "That's the Holy Ghost," says Saint Peter. "But why is he so sad?" At that, Saint Peter whispers in the sinner's ear: "Oh, he's sitting there brooding over that meeting in Nicea, where he was called upon to be the third person in the Trinity with a very slender majority and possibly the help of some cheating… He is, and this is between you and me, the only person who has ever become divine by vote. That's what he is so unhappy about."'

Lydia smiled:

'Yes,' she said, 'I remember that the Holy Ghost gave me a great deal to think about when I had to learn about all of this. God the Father was, after all, holy and therefore a spirit, and so was the Son. Why then did they need another "Holy Spirit"?'

'It may be,' said Arvid, 'that believers in those days did not imagine the Father and Son to be bodyless spirits. I'm not even sure, really, that they do today.

... The new June greenery surrounded them, and bluebells nodded in the grass. Bees buzzed, and the bells in the steeple were ringing for the dead person whose coffin had just gone by.

They often sat at her window in the twilight when the din of the city was so distant that you could hear the wind whispering in the crowns of the big, old trees.

On one such evening she said:

'Today I met him – the one I loved before.'

He didn't answer. He had been holding her hand in his, and he let it go.

'Don't do that,' she whispered. 'I didn't tell you that to hurt you. We happened to meet and walked together a few steps, talked a little about insignificant things. When I was alone again I couldn't believe that I had loved him once upon a time.'

Arvid's joy at those words felt like warm blood streaming towards his heart. But it was only momentary. Right after that he became very thoughtful.

They sat there in silence.

'What are you thinking about?' she asked.

'Nothing...'

'In other words, something I'm not allowed to know?'

'I'm thinking about something that might happen some day. But then anything that hasn't happened yet really isn't anything at all.'

She looked at him questioningly.

'I don't want you to think such ugly, stupid thoughts,' she said.

And they met in a kiss.

'Sing for me,' he asked.

She lit the two candles on the piano, sat down and sang Schumann's '*O Sonnenschein*'.

A couple of moths had flown in through the open window and fluttered around the candles while she was singing.

The summer continued.

One day in August, Dagmar wrote that his father was ill. His previously good health had been failing this year, but he had been up every day until recently. Now he was in bed and it was uncertain whether he would get up again. After all, he was seventy-four years old.

Arvid hurried to Lydia with the letter.

'Oh, is it you?' she said, surprised, when she opened the door to him. Then she added – with something hard in her voice that he had never heard before:

'I have told you that you may not come to see me except when I am expecting you. After all, I could be having a visitor, like Ester Roslin, or someone else…'

He stiffened.

'I have a special reason today,' he said. 'My father is ill. He might die. I have to go to him.'

'Please sit down,' she said. 'I'm sorry if I sounded hard. One should never speak that way to a loved one…'

She passed her hand over his hair.

'Is your father very ill?'

'It looks that way,' he answered. 'He is seventy-four years old and he has never in his whole life taken to his bed before.'

'Then you must go to him,' she said. 'When are you leaving?'

'Tomorrow morning.'

There were tears in her eyes.

'Well, that's the end of that dream,' she whispered, as though to the room.

He looked at her questioningly.

'I had looked forward so much,' she said, 'to this short summer for just the two of us – the two of us.'

'But, after all, my dear, we'll see each other again.'

'You never know.'

He took her hand and covered his eyes with it.

'No one has control over life and death,' he said. 'But I really don't know of anything else that could separate us.'

Suddenly, she burst out:

'Oh, Arvid, please don't go! Not now, not tomorrow! You can surely wait a little to see if it's really necessary. I'm absolutely sure that your wife is exaggerating your father's illness to get you to come!'

'No, Lydia,' he said. 'Her letters are uncomplicated and factual and don't sound like exaggerations or that she has other motives. Simply the fact that Father has taken to his bed shows that it is serious.'

For a long time she was silent. Then she got up and walked to the window. It was a dreary, grey day.

'All right,' she said finally. 'Duty calls. You might as well go! Goodbye!'

'Lydia,' he said. 'Lydia...?'

She suddenly weakened again. As she turned to him she said:

'No, Arvid, this is not the way we are going to say goodbye...'

She had large tears in her eyes and wrapped her arms around his neck:

'Do you want to be with me tonight?'

'Of course,' he said.

Then she whispered:

'Our life this summer, it'll never be like this again – never again. When you come home you'll have your wife and children with you. And you have your work and your friends and the people you work with: a whole world that is closed to me. The day will come when I'll be more of a problem than happiness for you.'

'Oh, Lydia, what do you mean? Have you taken leave of your

senses…? I'm going away, but I'll be back. I love you. Why shouldn't we love each other for ever and always?'

She smiled through her tears.

'No, of course,' she said. 'For ever and always. Or at least until the morning!'

He went to his office and made all the necessary arrangements there, then went home and packed his suitcase. Then he went out to dinner, and then on to Lydia.

The next morning he got up too late to make the morning train. He took the one in the evening.

Lydia stood on the railway bridge and waved her handkerchief.

The old man was dying, and he knew it. Arvid sat in a chair at the head of the bed, and they exchanged a few quiet words from time to time. The window was open. Outside, the smooth river Klara flowed by quietly between spruce-covered stretches of land. The doctor – the local practitioner, quite young, new at his job and unknown to Arvid, had just left. He had said that the end could be expected in a few days or a couple of weeks. His brother Eric had been contacted by telegram and was expected to arrive any day. Dagmar was sitting in a corner with some needlework. Anna Maria and little Astrid were playing in the yard.

The old man's thoughts were mostly centered on the lost son, the one who was sent to a foreign continent and disappeared, never to return.

'Do you think he's alive?' he asked.

'Hard to say,' Arvid answered.

You could hear the happy voices of the little girls outside: they had just seen their nine-year-old half-brother Ragnar arrive with his foster father Mr Ljungberg, the pastor. Big brother Ragnar whittled boats for them out of bark and told them fairy tales.

The pastor came into the room. Arvid offered him his chair at the head of the bed.

'How are you today?' he asked. 'Are you in a lot of pain?'

'I'm not in any pain,' the old man answered.

'Well, my dear friend,' said the pastor, 'I don't come to you as a pastor but as an old friend. We know just as much about ultimate things, you and I.'

'I actually don't think so much about ultimate things,' said the old man. 'I think more about those who are alive, those whom I will be leaving in this world, most of all about the one I know nothing about – whether he's alive or dead. I was too hard on him. At the time, I felt it was the only thing that could be done with him. But perhaps I was too hard on him, despite it all.'

He closed his eyes and seemed to fall asleep.

After the old man's deep breathing had assured the pastor that he was asleep, he addressed Arvid in a low voice:

'I don't come as a pastor to a man like your father. He has always been his own spiritual adviser. As a spiritual advisor, however, I sometimes visit the old poor farmers and their wives when they are near death. If they ask me, I tell them that this thing about "hell" is not as bad as it sounds. They don't always thank me for that. An old man who died a couple of years ago was furious: "I've spent this whole past year," he said, "feeling so happy that Olle Erks from Likenäs was in hell!" An eighty-year-old woman who died last spring confessed to me before she died. I can tell you about it since it didn't have to do with a crime, but instead a crime that was never committed. She confessed that fifty years ago when she was about thirty and married to an old man she was very tempted to give him some of that "white stuff". She also confessed – and this is what's most important – that if it didn't happen, it was because she was scared only because of this: scared of the executioner's axe if someone found out and of hell if no one did. She asked me if she would now be damned because of her sinful lusts and thoughts.'

'And you replied...?'

'I told her that no human being can avoid criminal thoughts and lusts, and that hell is for the living and not for the dead. She became white as chalk at this and raised herself up in bed: "I should have known that fifty years ago, when Erk Pers from Ransby was after me!"'

Arvid thought about it,

'This seems to indicate,' he said, 'that hell could have an actual "moral" significance for those who believe in it.'

'That's more than a little doubtful. We need only go back two, three hundred years to find that people in those days almost all believed in hell, lived and sinned just as they do now, or much worse. I had known the old woman in question for many years and knew that throughout her life she had been a splendid, fine woman. I believe that what really kept her from committing the crime was something entirely different, something she didn't understand herself, something that I cannot find words for, either. It is usually difficult to find words for such things. To find words for the essential, for what is really decisive... The longer I live, the more aware I am of this. And, by the way, this sort of a thing is very uncommon in my work. I must say that, in most cases, people in this congregation don't worry too much about "hell" even without my help. The peasants here in the countryside are just as wise as their pastor. And the Free-Church movement is diminishing. The Free Church people are dying off and many of their children are renegades: their childhood was so miserable and joyless that when they grow up and make their own decisions they make up for it...'

As he stood up to leave, he added:

'Värmland people are, as a whole, bright and quick-witted. If a report from 1634 is to be believed, almost every other peasant boy or girl in this diocese was already able to read and write by then. They have loved song and dance and music since ancient times. With this sort of people, Free Church movements and the fear of hell can become epidemic from time to time, but they never take root.

Through the open window they could hear little Ragnar's clear childish voice singing:

Manhood, brave and plucky men
can still be found in old Sweden's dens,
with their strong arms and plucky hearts,
youthful warmth, minstrels and bards.
Their eyes are blue, here and there

they smile in blooming fields where
they can be wild as a storm at sea
and mild as honey from a bee.

*

Arvid had only received one short letter from Lydia since his arrival. But in that short little letter there was one line, one sentence, that meant he couldn't part with the letter. He kept it on him at all times and, whenever he was alone, read it again and again.

During the past two weeks, however, he had heard nothing. Was she sick? Why didn't she answer his letters? Every afternoon when the mail came with his two-day old newspapers he leafed through them feverishly and stopped, full of anxiety, at each casualty or death… Once, he stared terror-stricken at the name Lydia in an obituary…but it was only a little girl of three months. In the same paper he read among the wedding announcements and personal messages: 'Walk by your window ev. morning. Could warm thoughts come true, your room would instantly be filled with roses. Lydia.'

He smiled to himself when he read that: the name Lydia, he decided, doesn't seem to be as uncommon as I thought…

Then his eyes moved to the announcement beneath: 'marriage: ASSISTANT MASTER wishes to meet cult. lady (pref. teacher) about 30, healthy (including teeth), medium height, musical. Answ. with photo marked "Sweden1908" to…'

Poor devil, he thought. Most likely he lives in some provincial hole…

And exactly under that stood the short notice: 'I'm coming at 9 o'clock – S.'

He thought: Oh, how many Boccaccio stories and Maupassant novels a writer could get together by simply reading the newspapers! Not that I am by any means a writer, and wouldn't really like to be one... No, anything but that!

Then he continued thinking:

What is this strange double life that I am leading? After all, it can't really continue in the long run. I love one woman and am married to another, and the other, Dagmar, doesn't have the slightest idea. This isn't the life of a normal man. It is a life which, at most, could only be condoned if I were a writer. A writer is forgiven for just about anything. Nobody knows why, really, but that's the way it is. Writers are considered to be less responsible.

He wasn't entirely free of the not so unusual and slightly contemptuous jealousy of the working and more or less unknown journalist towards those poets and writers who had a 'name': those who, whenever they condescend to write a little piece for the paper, are paid for their name rather than for their work, and who are talked and gossiped about and celebrate birthdays and anniversaries and soar in an evermore elevated space beyond all morality. They pursue 'experiences' for the sake of getting material for their novels and plays, then serve up the paltry bagatelles and banalities in which they have taken part in an adequately rearranged form so that they can be digested by a circle of readers...

Yes, most likely it is the life of a writer that I am leading...but I have absolutely no right to do that. I am a human being and a man – not a writer! I cannot stand it; it is against my nature. I can't stand living in daily dissimulation in front of a woman I have promised to love for better or for worse. I was unable to keep that promise and have already broken it. Therefore, I must tell her. Tell her that we must go separate ways: divorce. I must get a clear idea of my life, put my life in order. I can no longer stand this false double life...

When he got this far in his thoughts, his mind went blank. The practical details, what he would say to Dagmar and how all the arrangements should be made, not least the financial ones – all that became a confused chaos in which he could see no fixed contours.

He was sitting at his father's old desk. The door was open to the bedroom where the old man lay with closed eyes, breathing heavily.

Arvid sat there, playing with a pencil. He had a piece of paper in front of him. His thoughts were with Lydia, and he tried to draw her profile from memory. He felt that it did and did not resemble her. It was she, and yet it wasn't. He erased and changed and made new attempts. Finally he felt that he had really succeeded: it was she, it was Lydia, a living likeness!

He put the small drawing into his notebook and went out for an evening walk along the river. It had rained all day, but cleared up a little towards evening. The spruce-covered Branäs Mountain was mirrored darkly in the streaming water.

He thought about Lydia.

Where is she now, what is she doing at this moment? Is she sitting alone in her darkening room, playing Beethoven? Is she walking along some of the streets on which we last walked together? Or is she sitting at her window looking out into emptiness?

He took out the little drawing he had made a short while ago and looked at it for a long time.

No, it didn't look like her at all. How had he been able to think that it was like her? It wasn't Lydia at all. It was a completely strange woman.

He crumpled the page into a ball and let it flow away with the river.

*

It was the beginning of September. Days were cloudy and wet, the evenings long and dark.

It looked as though the old man was getting better. After dozing for days, he woke one afternoon and spoke – in short sentences, barely audible, but he spoke. He even joked. He said to Eric:

'Here, where I'm lying, I can see through the window that Ursa Major is going backwards, as usual. Which means that I am going forwards in comparison with Ursa Major! All motion is relative, after all.'

To Arvid, he said in a whisper:

'My dear boy. I'm afraid that you have a weakness for women. That need not bring a man dishonour, but it can easily pull him down, break up his career and close his way to the future.'

He spoke looking at the stars and in an offhand way, as though he didn't find it important. No one besides Arvid heard it.

About ten o'clock he fell asleep again and heaved long deep breaths.

Eric sat with him while the others went to bed.

Eric had sat up several nights already, and it is possible that he dozed off in his armchair.

When the house was awakened the following morning, the old man was dead.

Autumn was cold and wet.

One day in October, in the noon twilight, Arvid was walking up Drottninggatan on his way home. He was thinking and worrying about Lydia. Since the death of his father he had received one letter from her. It was short and to the point and rather conventional – it could be interpreted to mean that her thoughts were far away from him; but it didn't necessarily have to be read that way... He had not paid her a visit, since it was so important for her that he did not come when he wasn't expected. However, he had sent her a few lines to let her know that he was back in town.

Several weeks had passed since then. A couple of times he had walked across Johannes churchyard at the end of day, and looked up towards her windows. The first time they were dark. On the second occasion, there was a faint light.

He walked and wondered and worried about her. Was she, perhaps, already tired of her free life alone? She was mostly alone – apart from him, she associated with hardly anyone besides Miss Ester Roslin... Perhaps she longed for her old home, her little girl and her old husband who was so well educated and wise? Perhaps she had visited them this autumn, and hadn't wanted to tell him...?

He had arrived at the corner of Tunnelgatan. Tunnelgatan had always seemed to him the most awful street in Stockholm. Nevertheless, he turned the corner into the narrow, dark and dirty, stinking street, reeking with the smell of breweries, snuff-mills and whatever else, walked to the entrance of the Brunkebergs tunnel, went up the stairs to Malmskillnadsgatan, turned left and walked between two old tombs and some thinning trees across the quiet churchyard.

... No, there was no light in the window.

Suddenly he didn't feel like going home to eat. He walked to a cigar shop on Mallmskillnadsgatan and phoned Dagmar to say that he would be eating out with a couple of friends.

When he came out to the street again, he was suddenly standing face to face with Lydia.

For a moment they were silent and confused. Then she asked:

'Have you just been to my house?'

'No,' he said. 'That would be against our agreement. But I walked across the churchyard to see whether there was a light in your window.'

She didn't answer right away. They walked silently beside each other. They came to the churchyard.

'Well,' she said finally. 'Is it true that I mean something to you?'

'Do you need to ask?'

She remained silent.

After a while, he asked:

'Have you been in Stockholm during the whole time I was away?'

'Of course,' she said. 'Where else would I have been?'

They had walked on to a dark path and stood now in the shadow of the old red-painted wooden steeple.

She bent her head back when he kissed her.

And when they recovered themselves:

'I thought,' he said, 'that perhaps you had visited your former home.'

She smiled wanly:

'No,' she said. 'I haven't.'

The wind rustled in the dry leaves.

'Do you still care for me a little?' he asked.

Her eyes were filled with tears:

'Perhaps a little,' she said.

She took his head between both of her hands and looked into

his eyes:

'But you,' she said, 'should not care so much for me. It is perhaps foolish of you.'

'Of course it's foolish,' he said – for he had suddenly become radiantly happy. 'But, after all, the only fun to be had in this world is by doing foolish things!'

She didn't share his jubilant mood. She stared gravely into the dark and was silent.

He said:

'I thought I'd go home to dinner as usual. But what happened was I came here to the churchyard and stared at your window. It was dark. So I suddenly didn't feel like going home. Well, I probably would have felt the same way if there had been a light... But I went to this cigar shop and phoned home to say that I would have dinner out with a couple of friends. Anyway, dinner's unimportant. I suppose we'll go up to your place now?'

She seemed to consider something that was very important. She was silent for a long time.

'No,' she said. 'No, not now. Not today.'

'Why?'

'I can't tell you straight away. But I will let you know.'

He stood there, confused, unsure:

'Well, all right,' he said, 'I suppose I'll have to go somewhere and have dinner...'

'Yes, I suppose you will,' she said.

They separated with a cool handshake.

He went to the Continental for dinner. By pure chance he was shown to the bench that he privately referred to as 'Lydia's bench'. Later that evening he went to different places and met many friends and acquaintances. At the Rydberg he ran into Markel and Henrik Rissler. He felt a sort of antipathy towards Rissler, the reason for which he could hardly understand himself. He had never shown it, however, and when Markel asked him to join them he did so.

'My noble friend,' said Markel to Arvid, 'perhaps you haven't been informed of the fact that Rissler has changed careers and has now become an explorer? He has taken a trip to Copenhagen and discovered a new whiskey that is called "White Horse". You have to help me taste it – Rissler has already introduced it here.'

'All whiskey tastes the same to me,' said Arvid. 'I haven't had a chance to educate myself to become a connoisseur.'

'Then you must get up early in the morning and practise,' said Markel. 'But what happened to the rabbit?' he said, turning to Rissler.

'Are you a hunter as well?' Arvid asked Rissler. 'I didn't know that!'

'No, not at all. When I was twelve I managed once to shoot a squirrel with a slingshot. I really hit him, but when I tried to pick him up he clawed my hand so hard that I had to let him go. As I wasn't even able to subdue a squirrel, I gave up for all time trying to compete with Kaiser Wilhelm, who, according to Tolstoy, "lies in ambush behind a gate post in order to catch a hare". A few days ago I was at a dinner, and the woman sitting next to me was a landowner from the country and supposed to be quite a hunter. She asked me: "Is the hunting good in Östermalm?" I answered: "Yes, there's good sport to be had on the corner of Karlavägen and Jungfrugatan." She seemed to become a little thoughtful after that, and that was pretty much the end of the conversation between us. Later that evening I came in for some mild reproach from the hostess for having had a slightly obscene conversation with the lady! She had thought I had meant something improper! I suppose she had expected me to answer: "No, my lady, unfortunately we don't have any hunting in Östermalm!"'

'I suspect that, if nothing else,' said Markel, 'the very name "Jungfrugatan" can have certain unconscious associations, which might in some way explain the lady's misconception...'

Arvid sat, preoccupied. He was thinking of something else. Lydia. What was it that she couldn't tell him 'straight away' but would tell him later… What could it be? She looked so serious…

His attention returned when someone proffered their glass to him. It was Rissler.

'Skoal,' Arvid answered. 'By the way – there is something I have thought at times to ask you, but perhaps it is indiscreet, so you don't have to answer. Was your first book based on personal experience?'

'Not at all,' Rissler replied. 'It had to do with things that I longed for on the one hand and feared to have to live through on the other. Perhaps it is for that reason that this book impresses people as more true to life than any other book I have written.'

'That's right,' said Markel. 'You never lie so credibly as when you invent things. And reality is often so unbelievable that it seems made up.'

'Exactly,' said Rissler. 'But just that sort of credibility had sad results for me privately. I was very much in love with a girl at that time. I don't know how she felt about me: I never dared ask her. One evening, when I took her home to her door after one of Olof Levini's lectures at Stockholm University, I asked her how she had liked my book. She answered that she had not liked it at all. I concluded that she didn't like me either, and we said goodbye rather coldly. It was only many years later that the correct context occurred to me: she had, of course, thought that the book was a 'confession'. Since it had to do with a young man who had seduced two girls and had written a false cheque for so petty an amount as three hundred crowns she couldn't really have liked the book. The reviewers, by the way, had also written as though the book had been based on reality. It's hard to believe such a thing about those seasoned old critics, but they really did. So what can you expect from a girl of twenty?

Rissler took a large swig from his glass and continued:

'What I like least of all about Strindberg is that he has

accustomed the novel-reading public to always ask whom does he or she represent, and who is this one and who is the other, and how much is true? He has accustomed the public to believe that no writer is capable today of thinking up enough lies to fill a book. Since then it's been hell to write novels and plays. I just can't take it any more. I almost feel like writing a little book about what I think of the world – without making use of any imagined personages as go-betweens, without any nonsense or ornamentation. But the hell with novels and plays! Anyway, there is really only one mode of existence that is fit for human beings. That is to do nothing.'

They went on to discuss the Strindberg problem. At midnight Arvid got up:

'You'll have to excuse me,' he said. 'I have to go to the office and take care of the night's telegrams. Prince Ferdinand of Bulgaria has assumed the title of Caesar in its Slavic form: Tsar. I don't think this means anything special, but you never know... Goodnight!'

When he arrived at the office the next morning there was a letter from Lydia among the mail on his desk. He opened it and read:

Arvid,

I have given myself to another man while you were away. It wasn't love, nor was it 'the other thing' – oh, I hardly know what it was... But after you left I felt so lonely and abandoned by God and the whole world. I saw you constantly before me, together with your wife – finally it was unbearable. I had to find a remedy – perhaps it was also a desire to find out whether I could intervene in the fate of another.

It's all over now. It was already over before you returned. I don't think that you will want to reject me because of this. But it's up to you.

I wanted you to know this before we meet again. I could never have told you face to face.

Lydia.

He stood there with her letter in his hand, stunned.

No. It could not be true. It was simply impossible.

No, I'm dreaming... Or is this something she's invented in order to test me. Yes, that's what it must be. Next time I go to see her she'll look me in the eyes and say: 'My dear Arvid, did you really, for one moment, believe that it was true?'

No, that was even worse, even meaner. Besides, the letter spoke for itself.

It was true then. Real and true.

He suddenly felt sick. He crumpled the letter up, put it in his pocket and almost didn't make it down the corridor to the toilet. Then he threw up.

He sat brooding in his chair behind the large desk. He stared absentmindedly at the names of the world's newspapers: *The Times*, *Le Matin*, *B.Z.*, *Am Mittag*...

His first impulse was not to reply at all, but he didn't think he would be able to tolerate the consequence: never to be with her again. 'Nevermore'. No, that was completely intolerable. Unthinkable. It would make it impossible for him to tolerate living.

He smoothed out her letter and read it again and again.

'...have given myself to another man while you were away... saw you before me constantly, together with your wife...'

'Perhaps it was also a desire to find out whether I could intervene in the fate of another.'

What was that supposed to mean? In which person's fate – in mine, or in the other fellow's? You can always intervene in another person's fate. Any bandit can do that. Perhaps it's harder sometimes not to.

'...have given myself to another man...'

No, that letter isn't the kind you reply to. If I possess even the most infinitesimal spark of dignity, I will throw the letter into the toilet and never see her again – not even recognize her if I meet her on the street!

But still... 'Nevermore'. Never more... To pass her by on the street as a stranger walks by a stranger... Perhaps not even to greet each other...

I saw you constantly before me, together with your wife...unbearable...'

Suddenly he saw it: the way to retrieve what was lost. The bridge which led across the abyss. The possibility for reconciliation.

It had been jealousy that had made her betray him. Therefore, it was love. Why not, then, draw a line under the whole story?

He picked up a pen and wrote:

Lydia,

I have deceived you and have been deceived. I have deceived my wife with you and you with my wife. The only thing still missing from the symphony is that my wife would deceive me, and even then I do not have the right to complain. Of course, I had thought what was between me and you was something special, something unique, unconnected to the laws of retribution and such conventionalities. Of course, I didn't think that while I was burying my old father in the small churchyard in my hometown on a quiet September day, you were out having a love affair. But one has to be able to put up with everything. To take the world as it is even though it amazes one at times; and I must take you as you are. I will come to you tomorrow evening at nine if you will do me the honour of receiving me.

But I want you to realize one thing, dear Lydia: when referring to a woman's lovers, it is common practice to make use of the Australian aborigine's arithmetic: you only count up to three. What comes after that is called 'many'.

Arvid.

He reread the letter before sending it. Its light, ironical tone didn't really represent what he felt. What he really felt, he found, was impossible to express.

He left it as it was and he sent it.

After he had sent it, however, he read her letter again and stopped at these words:

'Perhaps it was also a desire to find out whether I could intervene in the fate of another...'

*

On the next evening at nine he stood in Johannes churchyard

and looked up at her window. There was a faint light. He walked up the four flights and rang the bell. No one answered.

He rang again. No one came to the door.

He rang a third time. No one came.

He went to a tavern and got terribly drunk.

When, during a later period of his life, Arvid thought back to that autumn in 1908, he referred to it as 'purgatory'. He had felt as though he were walking through a long, winding, subterranean tunnel, which became evermore narrow until he finally had to creep...and he found no exit and not the slightest ray of light... Suddenly he felt old. He felt as though he grew a year older every day.

The morning after he had rung Lydia's bell in vain, he received a short letter from her:

Arvid,

Excuse me for not opening the door to you yesterday. I had received your letter in the afternoon and did not feel like meeting you. Besides, a woman who has 'love affairs' on her conscience can, after all, not be right for you.

I was prepared for reproaches – but not for that. Now I want to be alone. Don't try and see me.

Lydia.

Pale and horror stricken he stared at the terrible words.

The day went on and it was evening before he was able to collect himself enough to write a reply.

Lydia,

My last letter did not apparently give you a correct impression about what I felt when I read yours – what I felt when I read the words: 'I have given myself to another man while you were away.' I felt sick. I had to rush headlong to the toilet with your letter in my hand. Then I threw up...

When I wrote my answer a few hours had passed. I can be easily upset but I don't carry a grudge. When I wrote to you I had actually already forgiven you. Who am I to judge you? I just can't understand how you can react so strongly to the expression 'love affair'. For that matter, what do you call it yourself? You wrote it wasn't love. Well, in such cases it is called a 'love affair'. That can't be helped. 'I was prepared for reproaches,' you wrote. I'm only glad you didn't expect compliments!

You can be sure of one thing: you will never find me standing outside your door again, begging wretchedly for your love. I had enough of that sort of thing the other evening.

Arvid.

After a couple of days that were as long as an eternity, her answer came.

Arvid,

Thank you for your 'forgiveness', but I have no use for it. You will never see me as a penitent Magdalene.

I did expect reproaches – but not ironic witticisms about love affairs and Australian aborigines' arithmetic.

I had never, ever thought that you could write such things to me.

Lydia.

Pale with bitterness, he read the letter, crumpled it up and threw it on the fire.

Bent like an old man, he walked the streets to and from work, his eyes fixed on the ground. He wanted to avoid acquaintances: having to stop and talk with them. One day he realized that he had walked by Lydia without seeing her face and without greeting her. But it was only because of fatigue and despair. He wasn't capable of looking up and lifting his hat. Besides, he felt that this empty ceremony wouldn't make much difference to two people who had been so close and become so far removed from each other.

He passed sleepless nights. He had terrible half-waking visions and fantasies. He saw her constantly: naked, with a naked man. The man had a head, but no face. He moaned in his half sleep. Dagmar often woke and asked him whether he was ill.

Often the thought visited him that he would die soon and that was good. That was the only solution to his difficult, confused life. He didn't think of the usual forms of suicide because he had life insurance and, despite it all, a small amount of concern for his family. He had, however, thought of a way to die that could not, from a judicial point of view, be considered suicide. When winter came, with snow and cold nights, he would buy a bottle of brandy one night, go to the outskirts of the city, to the edge of a forest, drink the whole bottle, or as much as he could manage, and lie down to sleep in a snowdrift. He was sure he would never wake from that sleep.

During the days he moved like a sleepwalker. At work he was an automaton. At home he was silent and cross. His enmity with Lydia didn't do Dagmar any good – on the contrary, he felt more estranged and indifferent than ever. Everything she did irritated him. Even if he had never really loved her, he had always looked upon her with approval. It was different now, since she had, without knowing it, become a living obstacle to the realization of his dream of love. He had somehow become estranged even from his little girls, Anna Maria and little Astrid. He caressed them absentmindedly and absentmindedly listened to their babbling and talk. One day, when he was rocking little Astrid on his knees, he surprised himself with this silent thought: what will you become, my child, when you grow up – a Dagmar, who lures a man into marrying her and then settles down with her prey, or a Lydia, who seduces man after man, never settling down until old age or death brings the supply to an end…?

For there was one thing he was sure of. That man – whoever he was – to whom she had 'given herself' while he was away had not seduced her but had been seduced. He was also certain of something else: that he had been younger than he was, perhaps younger even than Lydia. He didn't really know why, but he was sure of it. He didn't know who he was, couldn't even guess. That was probably why he saw him in his nightly visions as a young man with a head without a face.

From time to time, however, driven by something stronger than his will, he would go to the Johannes churchyard. He most often stopped in front of Döbeln's tomb. He would stand there and stare at it, he had no idea for how long. He would read the epitaph:

BARON GEORG CARL VON DÖBELN
LIEUTENANT GENERAL
BATTLES OF POROSALMI, SIKAJOKI,
NY CARLEBY, LAPPO OCH JUUTAS
TESTIFY TO HIS COURAGE AND HEROISM
IN DEFENDING HIS FATHERLAND

And above, surrounding the coat of arms:

HONOUR – DUTY – WILL

And again he would look up at Lydia's window. There was a pale light.

November passed. Every day, darkness engulfed more and more of this land of winter night.

One day in December, close to Christmas, he received some books from the bookbinder. Among them was the *Iliad* in the J. Fr. Johansson translation.

There was a story behind it. Lydia was actually the one it was meant for. Some time in the early summer – that brief, happy period, now so dead and gone it seemed as though it had never been – they had started to talk about the *Iliad*. She had never read it but wanted to do so. A couple of days later he had found a copy in a second-hand bookshop. He had bought it to give to her, but it had been a yellowed, tattered old volume, which he had to take to the bookbinder first. Only now had it arrived, bound: two light-grey leather volumes with a couple of simple decorations in gold on the spines – a helmet and a lyre.

Should he send them to her now? After everything that had happened since? She might see it as a pretext for his making contact, as if he were begging for love.

However, he had promised them to her. He wrapped them and sent them by messenger.

That same day he met her on Drottninggatan in the noon twilight. She stopped and extended her hand.

'Thank you for the books,' she said.

'You're welcome…'

They turned into a side street.

'To think that you bothered to send them to me,' she said.

He didn't answer right away. He was trying to hold back his tears. That was not something he wanted her to see.

When he thought that he could speak with a steady voice,

he replied:

'They were your books, after all. I had already given them to you last summer. The bookbinder didn't get them done until now.'

They walked on in silence.

'Well,' she said, 'I'm going home now. Goodbye.'

'Goodbye.'

The next day he met her again at the same time and on almost the same street corner in the same noon twilight and snowy drizzle. They greeted each other politely and walked on.

But in the evening he wrote her a letter.

Lydia,

I can't go on like this. I surrender unconditionally.

I still don't really understand you; maybe it takes time... You were so offended by my letters in October. But if I had taken the ugliest words in the Swedish language and thrown them in your face – I didn't do that, was not even tempted to do it – but if I had, how important would that have been compared to that single short line in your letter: 'I have given myself to another man while you were away'?

But you were offended and I ask for your forgiveness. You are my life. I cannot possibly imagine any sort of life without you. Cannot at all imagine that in the future the two of us will pass each other like strangers on the street.

You didn't want my forgiveness. You spat on it.

But I want yours! Forgive me!

Arvid.

It was few days before Christmas Eve when he wrote that letter. He received no reply.

Finally the snow came, exactly on Christmas Eve.

Arvid Stjärnblom had a day off. He had wrapped the small Christmas presents for Dagmar, the children and the maid and written on them early in the morning. Before, he used to think up short rhymes for the packages. This time he wrote only their names.

From early morning he roamed the streets in the light, white snow which fell and fell.

At a street corner he exchanged a hurried greeting with Philip Stille:

'Merry Christmas!' said Philip.

'Thank you, same to you... My best wishes to your wife!'

Philip Stille had been married for a couple of years to Elin Blücher. They had no children. They felt they couldn't afford them, Philip had once told him.

On Gustav Adolf Square he met Henrik Rissler. Absentmindedly he was about to lift his hat but changed his mind in time and nodded instead. After all, they had started calling each other by their first names that other night. Since then he seemed to like him a little better.

'Merry Christmas!' said Henrik Rissler.

'Thanks, same to you...'

'Do you want to join me at the Rydberg for some mulled wine?'

'Yes, why not.'

They found a bench with a view of the square.

'The façade of the castle makes a good background decoration in this snowy weather,' said Arvid.

'Yes,' said Rissler. 'People who didn't see it before the repairs ten or twelve years ago have simply never seen it. It was magnificent. It won't be like that again for another hundred years.'

They were silent, watching the shadow play outside, the people who walked by and stopped from time to time to wish each other a Merry Christmas...

'Tell me,' said Arvid. 'You have a Shakespeare quotation somewhere in one of your short stories: "I am so lated in the world, that I/ Have lost my way forever." Where is it from?'

'*Anthony and Cleopatra*,' Rissler replied. 'He had a devil of a time with a dark lady when he wrote that play, but he finally found his way home. Home to the small hole where he was born and where he wanted to die. And before that, he managed to buy himself a manor house and land and the lowest class of nobility, so that having spent his life as a comedian and writer with a bad reputation he could finally go to his grave as an honourable man.'

Arvid stared at the shadow play outside. He saw Kaj Lidner pass with his collar turned up.

Kaj Lidner was his Russian-speaking colleague in the foreign affairs department. He was a very melancholy man of about twenty-five. Once, last spring, he had told Arvid that all he needed was a decent reason to take his own life. He was very poor and had a hard time getting ahead. He said that he was a nihilist and an anarchist. Arvid remembered that at some time – wasn't it that Sunday in Strängnäs? – he had started to talk about him to Lydia. When he had told her about his talk of suicide, Lydia had said, 'Oh, that's only talk, of course. But what a beautiful name he has. Kaj Lidner. It sounds so beautiful...'

He was lost in thought. Then Rissler brought him back.

'When all's said and done, isn't it strange about this sentencing of Wicksell? An economics professor, already incarcerated in his youth for "blasphemy against God" and renowned for his almost pathological love of truth, suddenly suffers a relapse and gives a speech before an audience of young hacks in which he, perhaps somewhat coarsely, makes fun of the dogma surrounding the

Virgin Mary's virginity. What he said was not reported in the papers; they only refer to the fact that he said something obscene. Then half a dozen hacks of which not a single one – and I can't even make an exception for my friend Krigsberg – has as much religion in his body as the church weathercock, start yelling that this goes beyond all limits and that he must be prosecuted and sentenced! What sort of a court of law do we have? The law requires that he had to give "general offence" in order to be sentenced. But he did not give "general offence" to his listeners. On the contrary, they were jubilant! He gave "general offence" to Krigsberg and a couple of others! Or rather, Krigsberg and a couple of others saw to it that "general offence" was understood to have been given. That is what Wicksell is being sentenced for!

'Yes,' said Arvid, 'that certainly is a little strange...'

'By the way, how do you like working on the *Nationalblad* these days?' Rissler asked. 'Olof Levini is dead, and Professor Löök has taken his place. Gurkblad and Torsten Hedman have become too important to write for newspapers. You never see them any more in the *Nationalblad*. Markel has moved diagonally across the street to the *Dagens Post*. And Krigsberg replaced him! Doncker is the only man left in the boat from '97! "*Aber die Katz', die Katz' ist gerettet!*"'*

'Yes,' said Arvid, 'there have been a large number of changes since '97. But I have to leave now. Are you staying?'

'I'll stay a while longer. No, wait a minute – didn't Professor Löök write something about Pascal recently? Something about his being a master of scepticism? He has inherited Pascal from Olof Levini. That's the only thing he has inherited from him. Pascal, if one is to believe his sister's biography of him, never doubted, not for a moment, a single one of the "holy truths". He

* An allusion to a poem by Heine, 'Erinnerung' from *Romanzero* (1851), based on a boyhood memory. A cat had fallen into the water. Heine had asked a classmate to go out on a plank to save it. The plank broke and the boy drowned. 'But the cat, the cat was saved!'

was frail and sickly and in every way predisposed for religion. At the same time he was a child prodigy at mathematics and physics and that's the reason he has become, in recent times, of great importance and benefit to religion. No one pays any attention to a common pastor when he expresses himself positively about the Lord: that's his job, after all. But when mathematicians and scientists such as Pascal, Newton and Swedenborg do the same, then "our Lord's" followers understand enough to listen!'

Arvid roamed the streets in the falling snow.

Dinner was a long way off. On Christmas Eve they didn't eat until seven. He went to the Café du Nord to have some lunch.

At one of the window tables sat a poet and two comedians. Arvid took a seat at a table nearby. He heard the poet tell a story about his love life when he was young.

'Once, at the beginning of the seventies,' he said, 'I was very much in love with a girl who sold cigars on Näckströmsgatan, and we really enjoyed being together. Then another poet arrived and took her away from me, a poet with gold and furs! That was Edvard Bäckström! So I said what the hell and didn't think about her any more. But one evening I met her on the street and we walked a little way towards Skeppsholmen. There was the devil of a beautiful moon. I reproached her faithlessness. At that she stepped on to the quayside, spread out her arms and said: "I swear that I never in my life have loved anyone else but you!" Then she threw herself into the water!'

'Well, I suppose you jumped in after her and fished her out?' said one of the others.

'No,' he answered, 'after all I'd already had her! But I lay down on the quayside, and holding on to an iron ring with one hand, pulled her up with the other. Then I put her in a taxi and took her home to her mother. As I stood there and explained the situation to the old lady, Edvard Bäckström came in, wearing his damned furs. The old lady pointed to me and said, "This young man here has just saved Lydia!" So Edvard Bäckström moved his hand towards his wallet, but I said, "No, excuse me, Mr Bäckström, I am also a poet!" And then I left!'

Arvid had listened thoughtfully. 'Lydia'. So, there was a Lydia in the 1870s as well. Yes, I suppose that there's always been one and there always will be. She is eternal, like nature.

Again, he roamed the streets in the falling snow.

Something inside him drove him to Johannes churchyard. He was ashamed of it. But his steps took him there.

Again he stood at Döbeln's tomb and read the worn gold epitaph.

HONOUR – DUTY – WILL

Somehow, without his knowing why, his thoughts jumped to Kaj Lidner. 'It sounds so beautiful,' she had said about his name – he had come in to work at the paper very irregularly this past autumn, Kaj Lidner. During the last few weeks he had hardly been there. He had been ill, he said, and he really did look bad. Doncker had mentioned that he might dismiss him. He had looked like the shadow of a shadow as he walked by the Rydberg's window.

'Arvid.'

He turned around. It was Lydia.

'I thought I saw you from my window,' she said. 'But I wasn't sure.'

He was silent.

She whispered:

'Come up to me.'

He shook his head.

'No,' he said. 'It's taken you too long. You have tormented me too cruelly and for too long.'

'Forgive me,' she whispered. 'Now come. I'm asking you to. I am so lonely and desperate. This is the last time I will ask you, if you say no again.'

He went up with her.

They sat at the window. The snow fell and fell. Her eyes were full of tears.

'Tell me something,' he said. 'You wrote in that letter that you wanted to see if you had the power to intervene in another person's destiny. What did that mean?'

'Oh, nothing…'

'Anyone,' he said, 'can have that sort of power. Maybe one should be a little careful about using it, don't you think?'

'Perhaps,' she answered. 'But now we will let the snow cover all of that.'

'Yes,' he said. 'Let's.'

They sat cheek to cheek, staring out. And the snow, it fell and fell.

The *Iliad* was lying on the table. He asked:

'Have you read any of it?'

'No,' she said. 'But do read me something from it!'

He took the second volume and leafed through it a little. He came to Book 14. He read for her the lines where starry-eyed, wonderful Hera borrows Aphrodite's girdle in order to seduce Zeus and in that way win his interest in her political intrigues.

Aphrodite, lover of smiling eyes,
replied to her:
'It is not possible
and not expedient, either, to deny you,
who go to lie in the great arms of Zeus.'

Now she unfastened from around her breast
a pieced brocaded girdle. Her enchantments
came from this: allurement of the eyes,

hunger of longing, and the touch of lips
that steals all wisdom from the coolest men.
This she bestowed in Hêra's hands murmured;

'Take this girdle, keep it in your breast.
Here are all suavities and charms of love,
I do not think you will be ineffective
in what you plan.'
Then wide-eyed Hêra smiled
and smiling put the talisman in her breast.
Aphrodite entered her father's house,
but Hêra glided from Olympos, passing
Pieria and cherished Emathia,
flashing above the snowy-crested hills
of Thracian horsemen.

The lord of cloud replied:
But you may go there
later, Hêra. Come lie down. We two
must give ourselves to love-making. Desire
for girl or goddess in so wild a flood
never came over me!

It was getting dark. And the snow, it fell and it fell.

Lydia got up, passed her hand softly over his hair, took the book out of his hands and put it on the table.

'Come,' she said.

She went into the bedroom. She lit the two candles in front of the mirror. Then slowly, silently, she began to loosen her clothes.

Outside the winter dark had already sunk over the trees of the churchyard. The two candles glimmered quietly in front of the mirror

Suddenly the doorbell rang. They both sat up in bed and listened. It rang once again.

They almost held their breath. After a long silence the bell rang for a third time.

He whispered to her:

'You could at least show him the mercy of putting out the candles. Then he would be spared seeing the light in your window when he walks in the churchyard and turns around and stares up…'

She answered:

'Oh, he has most certainly seen the light already. It's better that he realizes once and for all that I am no longer here for him.'

And she let the candles burn.

She was still sitting upright in bed as though she were listening. But all was quiet. Then she asked:

'Tell me, what does "Ate" mean?'

He thought for a minute.

'Ate,' he said, 'was a Greek goddess. One of the lesser ones. One of the Fates. An unlucky goddess, she was seen as the personification of delightful depravity. Why do you want to know?'

'It doesn't matter…'

She rested her chin in her hand and stared out into emptiness.

He lay with his eyes closed, thinking. Why did she want to know about Ate? 'He' had perhaps some time called her that. Perhaps in a letter. He remembered now that there had been a letter on her table when he first came in and that she had hurriedly put it into a drawer. Suddenly Kaj Lidner came into his thoughts again. Lidner did not only know Russian, he was also very good at Greek…

'Tell me,' he said, 'why did you ask about Ate?'

She stared emptily into the emptiness and was silent.

The day after Christmas Arvid was back at work. The topic of conversation among his colleagues that morning was how Kaj Lidner had shot himself in Haga Park on Christmas Eve. They had found his snow-covered body on the steps of the Eko Temple on Christmas morning.

The funeral quickly followed. All the staff at the paper attended, and Dr Doncker gave a little speech at the grave.

In the evening Arvid went to see Lydia. She had not asked him that time, but he felt that he had to take care of her.

She opened the door. She was very pale.

'To think that you came, despite it all,' she said. 'I didn't dare ask you. I was so afraid of a refusal.'

They each sat on a chair in front of the dying fire. She stared with dry eyes into the embers.

She whispered:

'Were you at the funeral?'

'Yes.'

He noticed that she avoided using the name of the deceased. They were silent for a long time. Then he said, without looking at her:

'So, it was him.'

She lowered her head and nodded.

She was so pale and so little as she sat there hunched up. It was as though she wanted to hide and disappear.

'Oh how right he was!' she whispered. 'I wish I could do the same.'

He pressed her head against his chest and caressed her hair and her cheek:

'Lydia,' he whispered. 'Little Lydia...'

Finally the dam broke and tears rolled down her cheeks and she sobbed quietly.

'What have I done?' she sobbed. 'Oh, he was so kind and nice...'

'Well yes, but there are so many nice boys, after all, and you can't very well play with all of them.'

She buried her head against his chest and cried and cried.

PART V

'Nearer, my God, to Thee!'

There came a time of peace and calm.

The snow fell, a great deal of snow. Arvid and Lydia both welcomed it. Perhaps they both felt that more snow than usual had to fall this winter.

And he had a feeling that she had finally found peace; that she was no longer 'searching'.

She was so little that winter. And she was affectionate and tender as never before. He loved her more than ever and believed himself loved; many things happened that made this illusion excusable...but he no longer planned to divorce his wife for her sake and break up his home. Every time his thoughts moved in that direction he remembered what had happened – despite the snow that fell and fell... He left things as they were, letting them go as they would.

And never, ever, did she indicate by word or innuendo that she was considering a future as his wife.

On the contrary.

'I will never marry again,' she had said one day when they were sitting at her window in the winter twilight. 'Once is enough. More than enough!'

After a while he grew used to his strange double life, the way it had turned out to be.

Winter went by, and the sun returned, and the snow melted and it became spring again.

One rosy twilight in spring they were walking together among the graves in the New Cemetery. Lydia had bought a cowslip wreath from a poor little old woman at the gate. She wanted to put it on Kaj Lidner's grave, but they couldn't find it in this big city of graves, which was much more densely populated than the city of the living. So she put the wreath on her father's grave instead.

They were talking about dead people whom they had known. Arvid mentioned Olof Levini.

'I was once invited to his home, many years ago,' he said. 'And I'm still annoyed, to this day, that I was prevented from going on that one occasion. No one could have been kinder, more thoughtful or more naturally friendly towards us subordinate hacks. He was knowledgeable on just about every subject except the question of the Union. Once he said to me: "Can you understand what these Norwegians are making a fuss about?" "Yes," I said. "They're making a fuss because they want the first paragraph in their constitution to go into effect. The first paragraph in their constitution states that Norway shall be 'a free and independent state'. The situation, however, is this: the Norwegian ministry for foreign affairs is headed by our foreign minister, who is responsible only to our parliament. That is called 'autonomy', not 'sovereignty' or 'independence'. I hope our foreign minister does the best he can. Certainly we Swedes would not be too happy if our foreign ministry was headed by, for example, the Russian foreign minister, even if he behaved like a little angel of God." "No, is that really so?" Levini replied.'

'They say,' said Lydia, 'his death was actually a suicide, and that it had to do with an unhappy love affair. What do you think?'

'Well, I didn't know him that well,' he said, 'but I don't think it's true. He was a poet. I have spent a lot of time studying the nature and being of poets and have come to the conclusion that in the entire history of world literature it is hard to find a poet, a real and significant one, who has taken his life because of an unhappy love affair. They have other resources. They have the ability to release their suffering through poems, a novel, or a play. Werther is a case in point. Once, when Goethe had a tangled love affair in his youth, he wrote a novel that ended with the protagonist committing suicide. In its time, that novel is supposed to have caused a small epidemic of suicides, but unfortunately not among the poets! I don't know how the late Goethe felt about this; most likely he felt triumphant about having helped so many creatures unfit for life out of this world! He himself lived to become a judge, a minister and horribly old, and had a good and decent end. Olof Levini's death was simply an accident. If he had wanted to take his life he would not have chosen to swallow a glass of mouthwash, which only rarely works as a lethal poison. He had influenza and a high fever and, being thirsty and delirious, he drank the mouthwash. It so happened that he had a susceptibility for that not particularly dangerous poison. Another person would most likely not have been harmed.'

She walked silently by his side in the paling rose dusk of the spring evening.

'Poets,' he continued, 'are a special kind of people. I warn you to be careful! They are strong but often use weakness as a disguise. A poet can take punishment that would kill a common man. He does feel pain, but it doesn't harm him especially. On the contrary: he turns it into work. He profits by it! Look at Strindberg. It is not what he has experienced that is the cause for all that is sick, horrible and confused in his writing. That's what he seems to believe himself, but that's not the way it is. On the contrary, it is all that is sick, horrible and confused in his own nature that causes everything he has to experience and live through. However, which common human being other than a great poet could in any way go through what he has gone through and stay in one piece? And not just in one piece, but strengthened! All the bad things that he has lived through have been of service to him – as subject matter, nourishment, cure! As health almost. I saw him on my way to work one morning a few days ago. I can't remember ever having seen a man of sixty looking so healthy, strong and pleased as he did.'

Lydia walked beside him with half-lowered eyelids. The spring evening was getting pale and blue.

She said:

'I think, despite it all, you would very much like to be a poet...'

He replied:

'I want to be a human being and a man. I don't want to be a poet if I can help it!'

She walked with her head lowered in thought.

'But if you were a poet – could you not then do like Goethe and Strindberg and so many other and lesser ones, make 'literature' from what once was, for you, life and reality, happiness and unhappiness? Couldn't you?'

'Never,' he answered.

Their eyes met in firm seriousness.

He added after a while:

'I don't think that it's possible, for that matter, even for a poet to make literature from his love so long as there is a spark of life in it. I suppose it has to be dead first, before he can embalm it.'

They walked silently together.

'Since you wouldn't like to be a poet,' she said, 'what would you actually like to be?'

'That I don't dare talk about,' he said. 'You'd laugh at me.'

'Oh no,' she said, 'I don't think you should be afraid of that. What would you most like to be?'

'It's not easy to say with words,' he said. 'I believe that I would like to be something that most likely doesn't exist. I would like to be "the soul of the world". To be the one who knows and understands everything.'

It was growing darker and darker. The lamps were being lit in the inner city.

And the years went by.

Abdul Hamid was deposed in Constantinople at about the same time as the devil met a similar fate, with the appreciative agreement of the clergy, at a meeting at the People's House in Stockholm. Arvid's eldest brother-in-law, Harald Randel, was among them. Pastor Randel believed in God as a beautiful and edifying folkloristic conception from which people, including himself, could still derive much strength and consolation. The devil, on the other hand, he considered hopelessly antiquated. Nevertheless, he did not say this from the pulpit. He was one of the young, freethinking pastors who listened to Vitalis Nordström's advice: 'Only by means of a change in tone can you make much of the old thinking, which should have died long ago, wither away.' And the Shah of Persia abdicated, and the Russian Tsar and Tsarina visited King Gustaf V in Stockholm, and a young socialist, who, annoyed because he didn't get a chance to shoot them, shot a Swedish general instead... And people have started to fly! Blériot flew across the English Channel!

In January, a year later, there came a terrible comet with a long tail. One evening Arvid and Lydia stood on the Observatory hill and watched it. Later that year, Portugal dismissed its young and charming King and became a republic, and a big black cloud rose from Morocco, and the big powers showed their teeth and growled at each other, but no one dared take the first bite!

In his free time during the past two or three years Arvid had worked on a monograph on Chopin. In the autumn of 1910 it was finally completed and came out with rich and beautiful illustrations. The music public liked it, and it even went into a second edition.

'What would you like me to write as a dedication?' he asked Lydia when he came to see her with the book.

'Write what you want,' she said. 'Only do it in pencil so that I can erase it in case Ester wants to borrow it.'

So, he wrote:

Lydia at her piano, drones.
Chopin, beneath his gravestone, moans.

He could write that because they were such good friends that she could even tolerate a little teasing – something very rare among women – even though she really played very well.

On the evening of the same day they went to the Opera together. It was *Carmen* with Mrs Claussen. They both loved that opera, almost fanatically.

They did not sit next to each other, of course – she sat diagonally in front of him. And they didn't speak to each other while in the theatre.

Afterwards, he had to go to work. He first walked her to her door. Like so many times before, they stopped in the shadow of the old steeple. It was a windy evening in autumn. The moon looked pale and sickly as it hurried through the ragged clouds. The wind whistled through the thinning crowns of the trees.

They stood there in silence.

'At this point, poor Don José is being hanged.'

'Was he hanged?' she asked.

'Yes, in Mérimée's story...'

She thought about it.

'Can you understand,' she said, 'how you can kill a woman because she no longer loves you?'

He answered:

'She's destroyed his whole wretched life, after all. She has turned him into a deserter and a bandit. Besides, it is a very good feature that he has absolutely no intention of killing her at the beginning of the last scene. That was not the reason he had come. She drives him to it; she scorns him and provokes him in the extreme. She hits him in the face with her love for another. She uses it as a whip to hit him across the eyes. So he really can't help but see red. He is an ordinary man of the people and not a "poet". Had he been a poet, he would have saved Carmen from the knife and himself from hanging. Poets have other resources. Other vents and outlets.'

Then he added with a smile:

'A young poet, very talented by the way, and a young actress, who had been engaged for a while, broke up a few days ago. The poet immediately announced the broken engagement in the *Nationalblad*, complete with its causes and internal context, in the form of a poem!'

Lydia smiled:

'Yes,' she said, 'I read it...'

He took her to her door and they separated with a cursory kiss.

He stayed in the churchyard for a few minutes to see the light go on in her window. It did go on, but immediately disappeared when she rolled down her blinds.

She had finally acquired blinds.

These days, he decided, since man has learned to fly, you really need blinds, even on the fifth floor above Johannes churchyard...

★

For the first time since the divorce Lydia spent Christmas as a guest in her former home.

Everything is the same here, she wrote in a letter. *As before, the bullfinches sit on the frost-white branches outside my old window. As before, I play a little for Markus after dinner, in the half-dark drawing room. My little girl has grown and will certainly be very sweet. Markus is friendly and nice to me but doesn't talk very much. He has aged a lot in recent years.*

Winter passed, and there came another spring. In the early summer Arvid allowed himself the small extravagance of taking a holiday trip with Lydia to Copenhagen and Lübeck. They rode on the merry-go-round at the Tivoli in Copenhagen. They sat on deck during the light summer night's trip by steamer to Lübeck. The next morning they smiled at the amusements of Travemünde. Here and there they saw a stork standing on one leg philosophizing on one of the sandbanks of the Trave. At dusk they wandered through Lübeck's old winding streets and drank Rhenish wine in old cellar vaults from the fourteenth century. They walked under the old cathedral's two leaning verdigris copper steeples, almost a little afraid to have them fall on their heads – that's how much they were leaning! They stood and kissed in a window recess in the same room where, almost four hundred years before, the young Gustav Eriksson had spoken as best he could in Low German with the councillors of Lübeck and thereby succeeded in getting what he wanted...

In the autumn of 1911 Arvid published another book. It was called *States and People* and it came at a propitious time. It had to do with Swedish foreign affairs, their standing, prospects and resources for the near future. The thinking in this book, which took him historically back to his schooldays in Karlstad, was still relevant. There was other thinking of a later date. Sweden had, at that time, been seized with uneasiness about its future. The book consequently went into three editions within a few weeks.

On the whole he was successful in his endeavours during that year, which amazed him but also made him somewhat uneasy. He asked himself from time to time: how is it possible for me to be so successful? Maybe I'm a fake.

He had suddenly become a 'name'. Not a big name, but a writer with an intelligence to be taken into account.

For a couple of weeks he worked on a New Year's revue, which was accepted by the most important theatre director in the country, and on New Year's day it was performed at the Gustav Theatre. It was such a success that even the reviewers were impressed. Naturally he didn't attribute the main part of this success to himself. It belonged, without a doubt, to Ture Törne, the excellent young actor and singer: his irresistible sense of humour and beautiful voice were undoubtedly what was most important. Old connoisseurs from the eighties compared him to Sigge Wulff and rated him even higher. They also attributed to the revue itself a certain originality that was, perhaps, mostly due to the fact that its author, unlike his competitors in the field, hadn't been on a study tour to Berlin. On the other hand, he had borrowed a couple of ideas from Athens's Emil Norlander, Aristophanes – but no one noticed.

Lydia had also spent that Christmas in her former home. But she cut the visit short and was back on New Year's Day in order to take part in the excitement and happiness over Arvid's success. They sat in a stage box, behind a grill, while Dagmar sat at the front of the auditorium with her brothers Hugo and Harald and their wives.

Harald Randel, the pastor, congratulated him a couple of days later, when they happened to meet on Jakob's Square, on having written a New Year's revue without any tasteless indecencies. Therefore, Arvid had to conclude, the indecencies contained in his revue agreed with Pastor Randel.

★

Later in January, when it was apparent that the success was great and believable, Arvid gave a small supper in the Opera basement for Ture Törne and five or six of the other comedians and ladies who performed in the revue. Ture Törne sang Bellman – Arvid accompanied him at the piano – and he sang Emil Sjögren and all sorts of things, and he was irresistible. He took Arvid aside and said:

'It's hell this life I lead! I could spit upon my profession! I hate acting! I don't want to be a comedian! I want to write plays. I want to be a writer! And I will be a writer! You'll see – you'll see!

Ture Törne was twenty-four years old.

Arvid had turned thirty-seven a month or so ago. He answered:

'My dear friend, you seem to be suffering from the common curse of youth, which Henrik Rissler, by the way, has described in one of his books. It is that one dare not show one's real face as long as one is young. One needs to hide behind a signboard. You are a divinely gifted singer and comedian, but you want to be a writer instead. Do you really, seriously, think that would be so much better?'

Late one night at the end of February, Arvid came home from night duty at the paper. He was surprised to find that Dagmar was still up and completely dressed. She was walking back and forth and didn't answer his greeting.

'What's the matter?' he asked. 'Are you ill?'

'There is a letter there for you,' she answered and pointed to the table.

It was a closed letter-card. He saw right away that it was from Lydia. He tore off the edge and read the one short line: *I can't tomorrow. Lydia.*

He stood there with the small piece of paper in his hand, surprised and uncertain. There was an understanding between him and Lydia, which up to then she had always kept, that she would never send any letter to his home at such a time when it could arrive in the afternoon or evening, when he usually wasn't at home.

'Well?' said Dagmar. 'Who is Lydia? What is it that she can't tomorrow?'

'Then you've read it?'

'Yes, it wasn't too difficult. I held it against the flame of a candle. I can't think of a wife who wouldn't have done the same!'

She stood with her head high and her arms crossed over her chest, looking tragic. When she was very young she had been passionately fond of the theatre and had taken lessons from a famous actress.

They stood there silently for a long time. The ticking of the clock was the only thing audible.

'Well,' he said finally, 'now you know how things are.'

'And you imagine, perhaps,' she said with a smile that was

supposed to express contempt and scorn, 'that I will put up with your having a lover?'

'No, dear Dagmar,' he said, 'I did not for a moment think, or wish, that you would put up with it, now that you know. On the contrary, I sincerely wish that you won't put up with it, and file for divorce as soon as possible instead. I'll do all I can to make it easy for you.'

Her scornful smile paled and was gone before he had finished.

'Divorce?' she said. 'What do you mean? I didn't say anything about divorce…'

'Dear Dagmar,' he said, 'it seems you haven't, as yet, fully understood the situation. I love another woman.'

She wasn't listening to him.

'Divorce,' she said. 'Why should I ask for a divorce? You've been unfaithful, that's bad enough. But it's not so bad that I can't forgive you. Men are men, after all.'

'I'm afraid that you cannot simply forgive me in this case,' he said. 'Being forgiven implies repentance and improvement, and I can promise neither the one nor the other.'

She looked at him unsure, confused. Suddenly she collapsed. She threw herself on to the sofa and, with her head burrowed in a cushion, sobbed. It was no longer a pose, it wasn't theatre. It was only a pitiful woman who was suffering, and a man who was suffering because she was suffering.

He sat down on the edge of the sofa and stroked her hair.

'Don't cry like that,' he said, 'dear Dagmar, don't cry! I'm not worth that much crying. I can't ask you to forgive me in the way you mean. But I still ask you to forgive me for having hurt you. Perhaps each of us should forgive the other before we separate.'

She sat up:

'What do you mean? Have you heard something about me?'

'No, not at all. What I'm thinking of is this thing about our "secret engagement". You knew very well that I did not want to get married at all. You forced me into marriage against my will.

And a marriage that begins in such a way must, I suppose, always be a little delicate. Now we've reached the end of it. We should forgive each other our trespasses and then part as friends.'

She stared out into the room, horrified.

'You shouldn't say such terrible things,' she said. 'Divorce – why should we do that? Why can't we continue the way we have up to now? Who on earth is this Lydia?'

'How can we possibly continue the way we have up to now?' It isn't the way it was, since you now know how it is. You once said yourself that you wouldn't put up with my having a "lover". How then can it be like before?'

She cried and sobbed and cried.

'Oh, my God,' she moaned, sobbing. 'Why on earth did I hold that confounded letter-card up to the light! If I hadn't done that, everything would be as it was!'

'Oh, dear Dagmar,' he said, 'don't worry about feeling sorry over that. This could, after all, not have gone on forever. There is an end to everything. We have both deceived each other and now we can't live together any longer. Now it's late at night, almost four o'clock, and we are both suffering and tired. We will say goodnight to each other now, and try to sleep as well as we can. Tomorrow is another day. Good night!'

He wanted to go to his room, but she detained him there.

'Just tell me one thing first,' she said. 'Who is this Lydia?'

'My dear Dagmar,' he said, 'how can you imagine that I could answer that question?'

'Oh,' she said, 'do you think I don't know who she is? It's obviously one of those theatre hussies who're playing in your New Year's revue. It's Mrs Carnell.'

A Mrs Carnell, who had a small secondary role in his revue, happened to have Lydia as a first name. She was about fifty years old and no beauty even for her age.

He burst out laughing despite himself.

But Dagmar didn't budge from her obsession.

'Don't you think I can hear how forced your laughing sounds!' she said. 'But I know that it's her. You can let her know that my advice to her is to be careful!'

Suddenly he saw a protracted future of harassment and discomforts for the completely innocent Mrs Carnell. He said:

'Dear Dagmar, your guessing is all in vain. "Lydia" is only the signature she uses when she writes to me. In reality she has an entirely different name.'

Dagmar wasn't taken in by this improvisation.

'I'm not as stupid as you think,' she said. 'I know it's her.

She stuck with her fixation, since it satisfied her unconscious need to imagine 'Lydia' as a person who was in every way, socially, morally and physically, very inferior to her.

He said:

'It's late. Can't we now say goodnight to each other and continue this debate tomorrow?'

'I'm certainly not going to keep you from sleeping,' she said. 'That is if you can sleep! Goodnight!

And she went into her room.

He went into his room and undressed slowly, while listening to all the sounds in the flat and on the street. He heard his wife go into the hall and to the kitchen. He heard the water tap turn on then off again. He heard a cart rattle on the street.

He had no hope of falling asleep that night.

He had been lying awake for fifteen, maybe thirty, minutes when he heard a soft knocking at the door.

He listened and kept quiet. The door was closed and locked. With a key.

Again there was knocking at the door. As he stayed silent, he heard Dagmar's voice, weak and begging:

'Oh, Arvid – dear Arvid! Let me in! I can't sleep. I'm so afraid.'

He didn't answer.

'Oh, little Arvid, please forget about my saying such stupid things! Forgive me! I'm so afraid to be alone! Please let me in!'

He held his breath and remained silent.

'Oh, Arvid, I don't know what I'm doing! I'm going to kill our little girls and myself! I'm going to set the house on fire!

He had to let her in.

*

After that night he no longer slept in his home.

Most often he spent the night on a sofa in his office. Sometimes he took a room at a hotel in order to get a good night's sleep.

He had written a letter to Lydia about what had happened and how he was living now. She had replied. She was sorry that her wretched little line had caused him so much trouble. She could not understand it. *From the little you have told me about your wife, I had the impression that she was a woman who would be no more capable than I of reading a letter addressed to someone else.* Then she continued: *My little girl is with me now. She will be staying for a few weeks. Obviously we cannot see each other during this time. My dear, I don't really know how it is going to be afterwards, either. The more my little girl grows up, the more I realize how careful I have to be about my reputation for her sake. You have yours to think about. Let's bide our time – let time pass...*

He let time pass, and it did pass.

Dagmar seemed to have calmed down after her first excitement. Or rather, she had changed her strategy. She walked around humbly, quiet and resigned: a picture of the self-sacrificing wife. Since she had in this way managed to wheedle a promise out of him to try and spend a night at home, she left him in peace that night. However, the very next evening, when he came home late, she resumed, with a few variations, the whole programme from the first horrible night. It ended with his getting dressed at four in the morning and going out to roam the streets until five, when he found an open café for drivers and labourers. There he fell asleep in a corner with a bottle of beer.

⋆

In the middle of April that year there was an eclipse of the sun. At the same time the papers were filled with telegrams and descriptions of the sinking of the *Titanic*.

Arvid was standing on Djurgård bridge, and was watching the sun through tinted glass. However, his eyes tired quickly and he was more interested in watching how the shadows of passersby seemed to become paler and were finally obliterated and how ash-grey the light of the sun became as the eclipse increased.

'Well, if isn't it Stjärnblom! Are you standing here admiring the natural phenomenon?'

It was Ture Törne, the young actor and singer thanks to whom his New Year's revue had been so successful. It was still playing to full houses every evening – even though it was the middle of April.

'Yes...'

'Do you remember?' said Törne. 'Do you remember, last time, at the little party you gave for us in the Opera's basement – do you remember that I promised you that I would become a writer?

'No... Yes, now I remember... How is it going?'

'I've written a play,' Törne answered. 'That is to say, I still don't dare call it anything more than a sketch. May I read it for you one of these days?'

'Of course, but where should we do it? It's a little difficult for me to ask you to my house these days – spring cleaning and so on... Can you come to me at the paper some evening and read it for me there?'

'That's fine. But, as I said, it isn't really finished yet.'

'Well, there's no hurry, anyway...'

Ture Törne looked at the people walking by. Arvid was just exchanging a greeting with Henrik Rissler. Rissler had stopped not far from them and looked at the sun through a tinted glass.

'Introduce me to him,' Törne requested.

After the introduction, he asked:

'Mr Rissler, I am, as you know, a clown and a comedian.

But I've decided that I want to get ahead, and have now written a play. May I ask to read it for you? I'm going to read it to my friend Stjärnblom in a week or so at the editorial office of the *Nationalblad*. I would be very happy if you could come and listen as well. I consider your judgment very important.'

'Thank you,' Rissler replied. 'But, if only for the sake of courtesy, I must decline. The greater the genius a writer is, the less his ability to judge what others write. That's been shown by experience. Therefore, I don't feel exactly flattered by your finding my judgment so important.'

The eclipse of the sun had passed its climax. Among the many walking by was Lydia together with Miss Ester. But she did not see Arvid.

*

He ate most of his meals out these days.

On one of the first days in May he sat at a window table at the Anglais and looked out over Stureplan. He had just had dinner and was having coffee and a cigar.

He had come to a decision. He would write to Lydia and ask her to leave on a trip with him. Whether she said yes or no, he would be leaving, no matter what. Convincing Dagmar to file for divorce was hopeless. Since she had found out that he loved someone else she had been seized with a passion mixed with hatred for the man she had, for so long a time, considered her rightfully captured and self-evident possession. There was simply no other way out but to go away.

He remembered a short line Lydia had once written to him in a letter: *We two belong together.*

Well. So it was. So it had to be.

He had eaten his dinner late; it was half past eight. A golden-pink cloud was sailing across the light, somewhat greyish May evening sky.

He went to his office.

One of the boys in the hall informed him that Mr Ture Törne had phoned and asked for him.

Ture Törne. Yes, of course, most likely it had to do with the play he had written. After all, he had decided that he would definitely become a writer.

He picked up a bunch of telegrams and looked at them absentmindedly.

'How's Strindberg?' he asked one of his younger co-workers, who had come in to borrow a French newspaper.

'Apparently he's near the end...'

The telephone rang. It was Törne. He wanted to know whether he could come and read his play now.

'Please do,' Arvid replied.

A while later Rissler stood in the doorway:

'Is Mr Ture Törne here?' he asked. 'He phoned me this morning and wouldn't stop until he got me to agree to come here and listen to his play.'

'He's on his way. Sit down in the meantime.'

Rissler sat down.

'I hope the play is bad,' he said. 'There are enough competitors as it is... I seem to remember there is a small bar on the floor below us. Would you perhaps allow me to send one of the hall boys to get us some whiskey and soda?'

'Go ahead...'

The whiskey came up and immediately after it came Törne.

'Sit in my chair,' said Arvid, 'you can see better there.'

Törne sat down and spread out his papers on the table under the green lamp. Arvid sat down in one corner of the sofa, Rissler in the other.

'In your own interest, Mr Törne,' said Rissler, 'I propose that we have a drink before you start. That makes the critic "a little happier to start with".'

They drank to each other. Then Törne began to read.

It was a rough draft rather than a finished play. He made additions here and there and gave some information about the scenes that he had not yet written.

In the beginning Arvid listened half absentmindedly. Little by little he was seized by a strange feeling. A suffocating anguish. A stifled anxiety. His impressions of the plot and the scenes were weak and confusing. There was something else that he felt. He asked himself: am I dreaming or am I awake? He passed his hand over his eyes – it was ice cold – as Törne continued reading scene after scene.

The play was about a young woman – Laura von Stiler was her name – who is married to an old man, a historian and philosopher with a big name, and very rich. He owns a castle in Västmanland. And that is where the first act takes place. She doesn't love him. She loves a young officer who hates his murderous profession and feels that his real vocation is to be a writer. Her father is also mentioned. He is a painter with a worldwide reputation whose paintings fill a whole wall in the Luxembourg... He is the author's mouthpiece.

'I had thought,' Törne interrupted himself, 'that I would try to get Fredriksson to play that role.'

'He would certainly be delighted,' said Henrik Rissler.

Törne continued reading.

Arvid sat shrunken in his corner of the sofa. Here and there he picked up a detail that sounded familiar, an answer that he recognized... 'Laura (to her husband): Do you want to know the truth? – The husband (superior): I'm not interested in knowing it. The truth is harmful. Illusions and delusions have been the motives for all that is great in the world...' In one scene between

Laura and the young man she loves: 'I now know, Arthur – now that it is perhaps too late – that we two belong together!'... He also found out that Laura had two brothers; one of them was a judge and represented narrow bourgeois morality in the play, while the other one comes home from America in the last act with a great fortune, resolving all conflicts and problems...

Törne had finished reading. There was a short silence.

Henrik Rissler broke it:

'Well, Mr Törne, he said, 'it seems to me that you have some talent. What can one possibly say, however, about a play that isn't finished? What you've just read for us is nothing more than a rough draft.'

'Yes, of course,' said Törne, 'I'd already told you that in the beginning. What do you think of the conflict in the play?'

'Well... A conflict that can be solved with money... Of course there are many such conflicts in life, but it isn't easy to make them interesting in a play. And if I may make another comment, it is that your Mrs Laura seems somewhat unreal, a little constructed... You don't really believe in her. But be that as it may, I have to leave. I'm going out. Thanks for the reading, and goodbye.'

Rissler left.

Ture Törne measured the floor with long strides.

'What an idiot!' he mumbled between his teeth. '"Unreal!" "Constructed!" That's what he is himself! The truth is that I have created her directly from a living model! – but let's keep that between you and me,' he continued, turning towards Arvid. 'And don't ask me her name. One doesn't betray a lady's name!'

'No,' said Arvid, 'one doesn't do that. And I haven't asked what her name is, either.'

Törne added, somewhat distracted:

'I've had a relationship with her for half a year now. It's just about over, but we are perhaps going to take a little trip to Norway this summer.'

Arvid held a hand over his eyes: it seemed as though the light hurt him:

'So,' he said, 'it is almost over already…'

'Well, you know, brother,' said Ture Törne, 'one has to be careful not to get trapped! One has to live a little first, at least! Besides, in reality she is about five or six years older than in the play… But what's wrong with you? You don't look well at all! Cheer up, old man! Skoal!'

'Yes,' agreed Arvid. 'I really don't feel so well. But it'll pass.'

'Well, goodnight then…'

…'One has to live a little first'…'One has to be careful not to get trapped'…

A memory came to him, a shadowy memory: a ghost of a memory. He saw himself. He saw himself with his student's cap – one summer night, in a boat – once upon a long, long time ago…

Next morning at ten o'clock he rang the bell at Lydia's. She opened the door and let him in.

'You look terrible,' she said. 'What's the matter? Has something happened to you?'

He was unshaven and very pale. He had wandered the streets during most of the night.

'Well, yes,' he said. 'Sort of.'

She asked him to sit down.

'What's the matter?' she said. 'What's happened?'

He was silent for a long time, with his head between his hands.

'What's the matter, Arvid? Can't you talk?

'I'm going to try,' he said. 'It just so happens that I heard you are planning to take a little trip to Norway this summer.'

She stood there, as though petrified. It came as such a surprise to her that she didn't even think of denying it.

'Who told you that?' she asked.

'Is there more than one person I could have heard it from?'

She stood there, silent and confused. Finally she said:

'Oh, Arvid, get it over with! Tell me what has happened!

He told her the story. At the end, he added:

'I can't say that I recognized you in his Laura. Most likely two people don't exist who see a third in exactly the same way. But I did recognize the whole external framework about you and your life.'

She walked back and forth with her hands behind her back and her head down. Her long lashes shaded her eyes.

'Did he really say that he had had a "relationship" with me for half a year?'

'He didn't say your name. He is a discreet young man.'

'I really do know Mr Ture Törne,' she said. 'I don't know why I haven't told you about it before, but I haven't had any "relationship" with him.'

Arvid attempted a smile:

'If that is the case,' he said, 'Ture Törne will be a really fabulous writer some day, if he has his way…'

She came close to him and looked him deep in the eyes.

'Arvid,' she said, 'don't you believe me?'

He avoided her eyes, as though by doing that he could keep her from lying…

'Yes, yes,' he said. 'Of course I believe you…'

He found the situation demanded that he believe her. It would have been too embarrassing otherwise.

'If you really want to know,' she said, 'well, we've really only kissed a little. That's all. So it has become a play for him?'

'Yes,' he said. 'As I said before, in time he's going to be a damned good writer!'

'Oh,' she said shrugging, 'let's not bother with Mr Törne any more! One can't really take him seriously: one can't even be angry with him. But you look so worn and haggard, Arvid. Lie down here on the sofa and rest a little. If you want me to, I'll play something for you.'

He lay there with his eyes half closed. She played the adagio from the *Pathétique*.

Automatically he picked up a book that lay open on the table. It was Strindberg's *The Great Highway* and it was open at a place in which the author allows a misty pair of glasses to bear witness to a man 'who had cried a lot, but in secret'.

She had stopped playing. She came to him and laid her cool hand on his forehead.

'You are so warm,' she said.

'Were you reading this when I came?' he asked.

'Yes. I saw in the paper that he was dying. I took this book down from the shelf. I just like that part so much.'

'Yes, it certainly is beautiful. On the other hand, you can't really say that it was very characteristic of Strindberg to cry in secret. On the contrary, he has shouted and moaned and groaned loudly and publicly for the past generation. No doubt it helps. It helps a lot, actually.'

He got up:

'And now,' he said, 'I think I'll say goodbye.'

'Arvid,' she said, 'I suppose you have realized yourself that it can't be the way it has been between us. If, however, you still have any feelings for me and don't want to lose me, well...yes, then you can go through that whole long affair of the divorce and a new marriage and everything. Things can't continue the way they are now.'

He was speechless. It was the first time in all these years that she had talked of marriage.

Finally he was able to answer.

'Dear Lydia. I'm going to leave this place shortly, and I plan to be gone for a very long time. Yesterday, when I sat at the Anglais, after my lonely dinner, I had decided to ask you to come along – now, and forever. Since then, however, a piece of the moon has fallen down, it seems. Do you, yourself, really feel that this is the right moment for talking about marriage – after everything I had to experience last night?'

She avoided his eyes. He stood there silent for a long time.

'Well then,' she said finally, as if to herself, 'I suppose I don't have anything to save myself for...'

He felt as though, as in a dream, he remembered that she had said those same words once before – some time many years ago...

'When will you leave?' she asked.

'In about a week.'

'So...this is farewell then, I suppose.'

'Farewell.'

A few days later there was a letter from Lydia on his desk.

Arvid,

Forget what I said to you last time – about divorce and marriage. I was so confused after what you had told me, I hardly knew what I was saying.

You can keep your wife, as far as I am concerned. I have made my choice.

I love him – have never loved so much!

Lydia.

He crumpled up the letter, went out and threw it into the toilet.

From an open window across the street he heard a phonograph. It was playing 'Nearer, my God, to Thee'.

Arvid Stjärnblom finally found a little peace and quiet in his home... He had written to his brother-in-law, Pastor Randel – for the past few years Harald Randel had had a couple of parishes about twenty kilometres north of Stockholm – and asked him to invite Dagmar and the girls for a few days. He received a friendly reply and actually managed to persuade Dagmar to go. He made use of this respite in order to make the necessary arrangements for his trip. He gave the landlord notice. He arranged with Doncker to get a position as travelling correspondent. He arranged with a lawyer of his acquaintance to take care of his divorce should Dagmar be persuaded to agree to it. He didn't have the slightest desire to continue living with her: after his break up with Lydia, she had become even more unbearable than before. He acquired a passport from the foreign office. He packed his bags. Apart from his clothes and toilet articles he took along only a few books.

A pale ray of afternoon sun shone on the bookcase, where he stood taking out a book here and there and leafing through it. Dear old acquaintances and good friends. Oh God, old Ernst Friedrich Richter...*Manual of Harmony*, twentieth edition, Leipzig 1894... And Bellman and Lidner and Tegner and Stagnelius and Strindberg, long rows of them... And Olof Levini's last collection of poems, which he had so kindly given to him...it had been the year before he died... And Henrik Rissler: *The Life Of a Youth*. He leafed through it a little and stopped at a passage near the end: 'And if one day real spring-like sunshine comes into my life, I will, most likely, rot quickly since I am not used to such a climate.' Oh no, my good Rissler, he thought, you won't. You are most certainly of hardier stock than that.

He packed Bellman and Heine and an old French translation of Plutarch. He put his German *Büch der Lieder* into his small bag. It had been so long since he had read it. He wanted to read it on the train. He also took the Bible.

He was due to leave on the morning train the following day. He had written a few words to Lydia to inform her, so she wouldn't send any more letters to his old address.

He went out.

His steps took him to Johannes churchyard one last time. Once more he stood at Georg Carl von Döbeln's tomb and read the three words: HONOUR – DUTY – WILL.

As he stood there and stared at the three noble words in their fading gilt, he remembered three lines by J. P. Jacobsen:

Glowing night!
– My will is wax in your soft hand,
And loyalty a straw only in the blowing of your breath…

He remembered Lydia's last letter: *Never loved so much. Have never loved so much.*

Wonderful words, bewitching words when they are whispered at the right moment to the right person. Dirty words, shameless words, when they are spat out on parting at the one who is leaving.

⋆

The only thing left to do was to say goodbye to Markel. Markel did not know as yet that he was leaving.

He went to the *Dagens Post*. On the corner of Drottninggatan and Karduansmakaregatan he exchanged a quick nod with Ture Törne.

He found Markel in his office at the *Dagens Post*.

'So you are going on a trip?' said Markel. 'You're doing the right thing. It's certainly not too soon.'

He was holding a telegram:

'The Italians have been told off again in Tripoli, it seems. We live in a bellicose age, brother. "Lechery, lechery; still wars and lechery; nothing else holds fashion," says Shakespeare. And it's still true today! Well, goodbye to you, my boy! We'll meet again when we chance upon each other!'

He was buying his ticket at the ticket window. When he had received it and turned around, Lydia was standing there. It seemed to him, for a moment, that she was dressed for travelling. For a few millionths of a second the insane idea flew through his brain that she wanted to come with him – now and forever.

'I wanted to say goodbye,' she said. 'And I wanted to give you a little souvenir.'

She handed him a small package.

'It's only a little thing,' she said. 'A little thing you can perhaps make use of sometimes. And then you'll think of me.'

'Thanks,' he said. 'And farewell!'

He put the very small package in his pocket, went on to the platform and boarded the Southern Express.

And the train rolled on and on – southwards.

He sank into his corner of the compartment. Then he walked down the corridor and happened to see himself in a mirror. I am thirty-seven years old, he thought, and I look as though I were fifty.

He continued:

Neverthcless, I do want to see if a wider world exists – a world 'outside Verona'. I seem to remember that I once had the feeling that it did... But perhaps I have been confined too long inside Mount Venus to be able to survive in that world. It's probably too late now.

Then he thought:

It really was an awful habit she had, to always choose her lovers among his friends and acquaintances... After that awful autumn four years ago, when she wrote to me: 'I have given myself to another man while you were away,' I believed blindly in her sincerity. But was it sincerity, even now? Or was it instead a cruel desire to see how I would take it? A little cruel curiosity to see how much whipping I could stand?

He wanted to shake off all of this horrible speculation which he felt had gnawed at and corroded him for a hundred years. He opened his small bag and took out the *Büch der Lieder*.

He opened it at random and read:

In my life so dark and jaded,
Once a vision glistened bright.
Now this vision's dim and faded –
Once again I'm wrapped in night.

In the dark a child, dissembling
While the fearsome phantoms throng,
Tries to cover up his trembling
With a shrill and noisy song.

I, a frantic child, am straining
At my song in darkness here.
What if song's not entertaining?
Still it's freed me of my fear.

Yes, he thought, poets are lucky. They can find consolation for just about anything. Even if it is a devastated, burned up and wasted life, they can find consolation. They have the ability to express the hopelessness of their misery and thereby find consolation. But what is a common, everyday sinner supposed to do?

Then he suddenly remembered that Lydia had given him a present. A little souvenir. What could it be?

He fished it out of his pocket and unwrapped it. It was a little pocketknife with a mother-of-pearl handle.

At least she isn't superstitious, he decided.

For there is an old folk belief, which he remembered well from his childhood, that one should never give a knife to someone one values or cares for. It gives rise to hate and enmity.

He put it into his waistcoat pocket.

He thought:

Now she is most likely walking along a path in Djurgården to meet him. The sun is shining. She stops at a bend and says to him, with her eyes looking downward under long lashes: 'A little while ago I met with the one I used to love. I couldn't understand at all why I had loved him once upon a time.'

...And the train rolled on...

GLOSSARY OF NAMES, PLACES AND REFERENCES

The Anglais: the Hotel Anglais was a popular meeting place for writers at that time.

Edvard Bäckström (1841–1886): a writer of poetry and plays. Söderberg reviewed his play, *Eva's Sisters*, at Dramaten in 1898.

'Bellman trio': Carl Michael Bellman (1740–1795) was a unique figure in world literature, perennially popular in Scandinavia but almost unknown in the rest of the world. The lyrics for this trio appear in a translation by Paul Britten Austin.

Märta Brehm and Tomas Weber: the lovers in Söderberg's first novel, *Förvillelser* (*Delusions*).

Black Peter: Peter I, who became King of Serbia after the murder of King Alexander and Queen Draga in June 1903.

Büch der Lieder: *The Book of Songs,* Heinrich Heine's famous collection.

The Café du Nord: a lively café-restaurant located at Kungsträdgården, a small park in the centre of Stockholm, next to the former Dramatiska Teatern.

Mrs Claussen: Julia Claussen (1879–1941), an admired mezzo-soprano and alto at the Stockholm Opera from 1903 to 1912.

The Crown Princess of Saxony: deserted her husband and children and fled with her lover.

The Danaïdes: according to Greek mythology, the daughters of King Danaos killed their husbands on their wedding night and were punished in Hades by having to pour water out of bottomless vessels.

The Dreyfus Affair: the French Jewish Captain Alfred Dreyfus had, in 1894, been sentenced to a lifetime deportation to Devil's Island, accused of treason. In the fall of 1897 his brother Mathieu and Senator Scheurer-Kestner accused Major Esterhazy of being responsible. The latter admitted guilt later on, but Dreyfus was, nevertheless, considered guilty. He was not freed until 1906, after both Émile Zola and Anatole France became engaged in his case. Zola's *J'accuse*, 'I accuse', was published in the Paris newspaper *L'Aurore*. The Swedish translation, appearing in *Svenska Dagbladet*, was called historical and was an initiative of Söderberg's.

Femtåberget: literally meaning 'The Five Toe Mountain', it is a mountain near Arvid's home, named after the river Femte, which means 'fifth river'.

Gustav Fröding (1860–1911): a famous Värmland poet.

Erik Gustav Geijer: a famous nineteenth-century Swedish writer.

The Ghost Castle: a building on Drottninggatan used by Stockholm University.

The Great Exhibition: the Stockholm Industrial Exhibition of 1897, for which the architect Fredrik Liljekvist designed a reconstruction of sixteenth-century Stockholm in Djurgården, a Stockholm park.

Torsten Hedman: the playwright and critic, Tor Hedberg

(1862–1931).

Ellen Hej: the writer, Ellen Key (1849–1926). The name is humorous, being the Swedish word for the greeting 'Hi!'.

Mme Humbert: Thérèse Humbert, a French racketeer, exposed and arrested in Madrid in December 1902.

Jörgen: pen name for Georg Filip Lundström (1838-1910), publisher of the *Figaro*, on which Söderberg worked in his youth.

Jungfrugatan: means 'The Virgin's Street'.

Olof Levini: the poet Oscar Levertin (1862-1906). He was one of the leading critics on *Svenska Dagbladet*.

'The Lost Son': painting by Von Rosen (1885).

The Masters of the Kingdom: Sweden's 'rikets herrar'. In 1897 they were Prime Minister Erik Gustaf Boström, Minister of Justice Ludvig Annerstedt and War Minister Axel E. Rappe.

Mount Venus: '…confined too long inside Mount Venus…' is a reference to Tannhäuser used in a poem by Heine and also by Wagner in his opera.

'Nearer, my God, to Thee!': psalm said to have been played by the orchestra on board the *Titanic* as it sank in the North Atlantic Ocean on its maiden voyage in 1912. More than 1500 passengers were drowned. Söderberg chose the title of this psalm for his last chapter because it evoked an atmosphere of destruction and broken illusions.

Nordisk Familjebok: Swedish equivalent of *Who's Who*.

Emil Norlander (1865–1935): Swedish writer known, among other things, for his Stockholm revues at the start of the twentieth century. His New Year revue for 1905, *Stockholms Luft* based on the Berlin revue *Berliner Luft*, was reviewed by Söderberg.

Vitalis Norström (1856–1916): Swedish theologian. The debate to which Söderberg refers when quoting Norström took place in February and March 1900 and was sparked off by the publication of a book on Christianity by A. Nyström, which called for a rejection of Church dogma on the subject of Satan.

Adam Gottlob Oehlenschläger (1779-1850): Danish poet.

Henrik Rissler: an ironic self-portrait of Hjalmar Söderberg, who published *Förvillelser* (*Delusions*) in 1895 and started to work for *Svenska Dagbladet* in 1897.

The Rydberg: located on Gustav Adolf Square, it was, from 1857 to 1914, one of Stockholm's most elegant hotels and restaurants. At present it is a writers' meeting place situated on Drottninggatan.

Viktor Rydberg (1828–1895): a famous poet.

Henry Steel: financier, art collector and Söderberg's friend, Ernest Thiel (1859- 1947), whose collection can be seen today at the Thielska Galleriet in Djurgården.

Carl Snoilsky (1841–1903): Swedish poet.

'The Union': established between Sweden and Norway in 1814, at the end of the Napoleonic Wars, the Union was beginning to collapse in the 1890s amid grave political crises. It was finally dissolved in 1905.

Värmland: province in western Sweden and Arvid Stjärnblom's birthplace.

When We Dead Awaken: play by Henrik Ibsen (1899) in which the demands of love and life are forced to give way to art. Taunitzer Lake is a fictional symbol for life's finest hour.

GENERAL NOTE

There are many place names referred to in *The Serious Game* and they are often important to the text. Most of these places still exist today. The following information may therefore be helpful:

The 'gata' ending means 'street'.
'Gård' means 'yard' or 'park', for example: Djurgården.
'Bro' means 'bridge', for example: Skeppsbron.